Flown in for Christmas

A steamy, fake engagement, holiday romance

A. Boss

PEAK EVEREST PUBLISHING

To the friends and family who supported me through my treatment and continue to show up in the aftermath.

"Life is 10% what happens to us and 90% how we react to it."

Joy

"DAVIS BOUGHT THOSE SLACKS a size too small, wouldn't you say?" Lisa whispers, jabbing my elbow sharply. She's the lead from marketing, and quite the lover of office gossip, if I do say.

She's not wrong. His fitted black suit seems to be tailored a little tighter than usual, but then again, he *has* been using his private gym a bit more aggressively the last two weeks.

Water cooler gossip says it's his *stress relief* during the holidays.

Of which, he hates—the holidays, that is.

A modern Grinch, as they say.

I can attest to witnessing his humbug attitude myself. Between his demands I work late, including weekends—because if he's here, so should I—to blowing a head gasket when the littlest things don't go quite his way.

My face heats as I take in the tall, broad frame of our CEO. We stand off to the side as Mr. Davis gives his expected company speech on behalf of Davis Sporting Goods.

"He looks...nice," I say quietly, subtly rubbing the ache from my elbow.

Lisa snickers over the rim of her eggnog. "Ah, yes, a fine mixture of boy next door meets hunky Cavill." She sighs wistfully at the very mention of her favorite British actor.

I suppress a laugh as Mr. Davis raises his short glass of amber liquid, addressing the room with a warm, "Here's to another successful year for Davis Sporting Goods!"

The room breaks out in a resounding *cheers*, raising their glasses of wine, liquor, and spiked eggnog, while I sip my water.

I've got a late flight to catch in just a few hours. I can't be hammered going through TSA. One good swig of that eggnog and I know I would be. I'm the walking definition of a lightweight.

The crowd disperses to enjoy the rest of the party as Mr. Davis breaks off with his CFO, Richard Hanes. I keep note of my boss' whereabouts in case he needs anything. I was hired nearly three months ago by the advertising department as a promotions assistant. An extra set of hands to help run the busiest time of the year in retail: the holidays.

Black Friday, Cyber Monday, Christmas Specials. In-store and online doorbuster deals.

We sell anything and everything sports-related that you can imagine—gear, equipment, apparel, memorabilia, footwear. The

DSG brand is worn by the greatest in the NFL, NBA, NHL, and MLB.

Even with the holiday rush, someone in HR decided I didn't have enough to do, and added 'personal assistant to the CEO' to my workload, bringing on a *massive* list of duties on top of it.

Why me? I haven't the slightest idea.

It's not like I could say *no*. He's the C-E-O. And I'm still working through my ninety-day probationary period. There was no feasible way I could turn it down. I suppose I should be grateful for the opportunity, but...it's been a crazy few months, to say the least.

I smooth a hand down my shimmery red skirt, adjust the dip of cleavage in my black blouse, and toss my long, brown waves over my shoulder. "Any big holiday plans for you and Joe this year?" I ask Lisa.

She shrugs, her blonde bob bouncing as she sips her glass. "Family crap, you know the drill." She downs the remainder of her eggnog and I fight back the urge to gag at how thick that drink is and how fast she just did that. *She'll be feeling that tomorrow.*

"I'd slow down if I were you," I tell her. "Whoever made that went *heavy* on the rum."

"I know." She smiles wide. "It was me."

Of course, it was. We share a laugh, making our way to the buffet catering. The ten-minute alarm I set on my phone goes off in my purse, warning me that I need to start my goodbyes if I want to catch my scheduled cab to the airport.

"You're spending Christmas with your brother, right?" Lisa asks, watching as I fish my phone out.

"Yep. Spending the whole week with him." I smile at the thought of it. It's been *years* since Emmett and I made plans like this. "I had to book a few connecting flights to get through the holiday chaos, but I'll get to LAX by tomorrow morning. Fingers crossed."

She nods absently, glancing over my shoulder. "Don't look now, but Scrooge the Handsome is on his way."

I turn and my heel catches on itself, causing me to promptly lose my balance. I sway, nearly taking a tumble when a strong hand grabs my arm, pulling me into a heated, hard chest. An air of a masculine cologne envelopes me and I melt against my rescuer.

"Miss Bell." His deep baritone rumbles.

My mouth goes dry. *Mr. Davis.*

I right my feet, clear my throat, and stand stiffly against the heat radiating between us. I look up, internally scolding myself for picking my higher black heels as Mr. Davis' dark, sultry gaze meets mine. Dammit. "Sorry, I must have misstepped," I push out, plastering on a grateful smile. "Thank you."

Mr. Davis grunts, releasing my arm. His dark chestnut hair is styled tight in a slicked-back look and pairs nicely with his strong, ticking jaw covered in a dusting of a five o'clock shadow. He gazes down at me from his towering six-foot-three—and I feel a tense crick in my neck staring at him from this angle.

It's been a while since I've been *this* close to him. The last week he had been stuck in his office going over end-of-the-year reports.

It's not surprising a man like Mr. Davis hit that billion-dollar mark rather quickly when he took the reins. He's a man who tolerates zero runaround from anyone and commands the space and people who surround him.

He was a tight end in college—or so I've heard.

Ha. *Tight end.*

"I need you to send Hanes those promotion sale reports you updated this morning," he tells me. Molten chocolate eyes sear into me.

"Oh, yes, of course," I say. "I can take care of that now." Quickly turning to Lisa, I add, "I'll see you...next year." I laugh at my lame joke.

Lisa snort-chuckles, shaking her head. "Oh, god, Joy. Don't, please." She waves me off. "I'll call you. Fly safe."

I smile, scurrying toward the door when a weighted presence looms behind me. Glancing over my shoulder as I gather my coat from my seat and head for the door. Mr. Davis follows. "You don't need—"

He huffs, cutting me off to reach ahead and open the door to exit the banquet hall. I walk to the elevators with Mr. Davis at my side. We're alone as we step into the elevator. We rarely are. I mean, we've been working together for *months* but never quite so...alone. I hit the button for the top floor.

The silence between us is loud, but not as uncomfortable as I would've expected it to be. I'd imagine everyone working retail, whether that's in the company offices or in-store, is burnt out this year.

"Where are you flying?" he asks.

The question catches me so off guard it takes a moment to register he's talking *to* me. I don't think he's ever asked me a question that didn't pertain to work.

"Oh, um, California," I reply, shifting on my heels. "LA to be specific."

He nods. Not bothering to ask me who's in California or what my holiday plans are. I feel a little sad he doesn't, though I shouldn't. "Do you have any exciting plans for the holiday break?"

The elevator dings as we reach the top floor at the same time he replies, "Going to see family."

I smile at that, walking beside him until we reach my desk outside his office. "That's nice."

He strides past me without another word.

It takes me a few minutes to boot up my desktop and send the requested reports to Mr. Hanes. Once I'm done, I shut down and tug on my coat before I peek into his office from the open doorway. "Do you need anything else before I head out, sir?"

He's seated behind his desk, his chair turned toward the floor-to-ceiling windows to gaze out over busy downtown Dallas. He has his cell phone in hand, tapping it on his bristled chin, seeming lost in his thoughts. "No."

I bite my lip. He looks so...sad?

Sad and handsome and I wish, just for a moment, that he'd open up and tell me what's bothering him. He works so hard; he should be enjoying all he has accomplished.

"Well, if you need me, don't hesitate to call," I say, pausing for a beat. "Merry Christmas, Mr. Davis."

He doesn't reply. Nor spare me a second glance as I sigh to myself and walk away to enjoy my hard-earned, two-week—ten-business-day—vacation.

Sand in my toes, I think to myself.

That's what I need this Christmas.

Two.

Nick

I LEAN BACK IN my office chair, listening to the retreating tap of Miss Bell's heels as she takes her leave. She's been a good addition to the team. Smart and...pretty. She's easy to be around. I prefer her company over most these last few months.

I stare at the busy, bright lights of Dallas. The world feels...distracted with a mere five days until Christmas. Miss Bell isn't the only one traveling this year for the holidays.

I've got a 6:00 AM flight tomorrow to my hometown—North Tree, Wisconsin. Holidays have always been a big deal in the Davis family. Hell, *family* has been the most important concept drilled into me my entire life.

I missed Thanksgiving this year and I made the mistake of using 'work' as an excuse.

And now I'll never hear the end of it from my stickler of a mother.

I can't blame her for being so hard on me. I was the only one who didn't make it. Even Rich, my cousin and CFO, made it home. But not me. I've been putting this off as long as I can. Hoping and wishing the truth wasn't reality, but it is.

This very well might be my father's last Christmas.

He was diagnosed six months ago with stage four pancreatic cancer. At the time, his doctors gave him eight to twelve months to live, maybe more if he responded well to treatment. Thankfully, he has. But that'll only add time to his plate, the long-term survival rates for his stage are low.

And the cure rates...even lower.

I've been CEO of Davis Sporting Goods for the last ten years and 'acting president' for the last five. Ever since my sister, Natalie, started her family back in Wisconsin with her wife, Martina, five years ago, my father spends more time at home with the grandkids than working. I understand, he's always been a family man through and through.

Something I'm grateful for now. Being able to look back at how he was there for...well, everything. Every life event, big or small, he was there. My mother, too.

Football games, fundraisers, scouting events, bailing me out of jail when I got arrested for being a rowdy teenager climbing the local water tower to smoke weed with my friends. The list is endless. And it tortures me to think about his life coming to an end.

He's my father. The man I've looked up to my entire life.

The thought of losing him has been a hard pill to swallow and, I admit, I haven't been handling the situation the way I should be. I'm on edge and I haven't been sleeping well these last few months.

My phone rings, bringing me back. It's my sister, *again*. I ignore the call, whatever she has to say will just have to wait until I get there tomorrow.

"There you are," Rich calls out, strolling into my office. "I figured I'd find you hiding out in here." Rich is family on my mother's side, my Aunt Sara's son. Only a few people here know we're first cousins—considering the differing last names and the fact we don't look much alike.

He's a good man. I'm glad to have him as a trusted family member working with me.

"I had my assistant send you those reports we discussed."

He moves to gaze at downtown alongside me. Pushing his hands in his grey slacks, he nods. "Eric is bringing Darcy to, uh, Christmas this year."

I snarl under my breath, but steel my features.

Fucking Eric.

My late Uncle's bastard son who just *magically* showed up out of nowhere two years ago. He didn't wait get to know his long-lost relatives before asking about his 'rightful cut' of the family business. The snake slithered his way into the family by the good grace of my parents.

My father started Davis Sporting Goods as a family-owned and operated business with his brother, my Uncle Steve. Originating in Wisconsin, their beloved company grew to unforeseeable heights over the last four decades. Unfortunately, Uncle Steve passed away suddenly four years ago in a car accident, shocking my father and the rest of the family. Dad and Uncle Steve always ran the company together and made a promise early on that no matter what, DSG would be run by *family*.

He's kept that promise by handing everything over to me.

"Who told you that?" I ask him.

"Natalie," he says. "She's been trying to call you and give you a heads up before you're met with your ex-girlfriend on the arm of your biggest rival."

I grit my teeth at that statement. "Eric is *not* my biggest rival. He's a fucking sleazeball who wants everything without working for it."

It's true, he and my ex-girlfriend, Darcy, have been together for the last year and a half. She's just like him. Nothing was ever good enough, and she always wanted *more*. More money, more clothes, fancier dinners. They're made for each other as far as I'm concerned.

I'm getting ready to have the hardest Christmas in my life. Darcy and Eric are the last things I need to be wasting my time thinking about.

Rich nods slowly, looking me over. "You think he's just trying to get in good with Uncle Bruce? You know how your dad feels about family."

I inhale deeply. "Wouldn't surprise me." Eric hasn't made it a point to attend many family gatherings. He's just...there, sitting on the sidelines. Waiting for the right time to strike. And with my father's diagnosis, the snake has been moving in for the kill. "Dad's been on my ass the last few years about settling down. If that's the image Eric is trying to portray to get in his good graces, maybe that's why he's showing up this year."

"I've got your back," my cousin tells me. "However you want to handle the situation. I know you're going through a lot with your—"

"Don't," I cut him off and stand. I don't need his pity. Besides, my father is his uncle, he'll be losing him, same as me.

There is enough shit being taken from me. Over my dead body will I let *Eric Davis* take my father's company and sell it off piece by piece. And I'm certain that's what he'd do, he's voiced it as a 'money-making strategy' to me. I doubt that's changed.

I'd like to think my father isn't *that* naïve to Eric's end game, but Dad's gotten caught up in the aspect of 'family' a time or two. When I've tried to voice my concerns, the conversation always turns into a speech about family *this* and family *that*.

Blood might be thicker than water, but not even blood can make everyone family.

I stride toward the door. "I better head out. We've got an early flight and I haven't even packed."

Rich follows me out. "Leah's pretty nervous about flying. She's been so nauseous with the pregnancy. She's worried she's going to blow chunks mid-air."

I chuckle low, shaking my head. "It's a straight flight, shouldn't be too bad. But just in case, she's sitting with you."

We land at the Green Bay airport right on time. Rich and I pick up our rental SUV to start on the twenty-minute drive north to my parents' place. The temperature is at record lows according to the rental attendant. Negative fifteen degrees Fahrenheit with four feet of solid, packed snow on the ground.

It's not long before myself, Rich, and his wife, Leah, turn onto the long, barely plowed drive of my parents' house. They've upgraded quite a bit over the years. Dad was reluctant to sell the home they raised my sister and me in, but Mom sure wasn't. She loves the sprawling, wooded property with ten thousand square feet of rustic homage sitting on thirty acres.

Plenty of room for *everyone*. Unfortunately.

The place is decorated to the nines in Christmas décor as usual. I pull in beside the three-bay garage, sure to park in a way I can get out easily if need be. Before I even have the trunk open to get our luggage, Mom whips the front door open with a cheery shout, "You made it." She beams, shuffling over in her slippers and bathrobe through the crunchy, iced-up snow.

"Mom! Get in the house," I holler. "It's freezing out here."

Completely dismissing me, she sidles up and hauls me into one of her tight hugs. "Oh, hush. It's been too long. I missed you this past Thanksgiving, you know."

I bite back a sigh. How could I forget?

Rich and I gather the luggage, while Leah ushers Mom into the house. It's a good bit of *welcome home, we missed you,* and *who's hungry* before we finally take our coats off. It's barely noon, and I'm already beat.

I feel like I'm running on fumes having not slept last night.

After I take my luggage upstairs to my room, I head for the kitchen. Natalie is waiting for me with my newest adopted niece, Izzy. She's a newborn, barely a month old. You would think holding a tiny baby would tamp down some of the heat in my sister's glare, but it doesn't.

"Do I need to kick your ass so you'll start answering my calls?" she whisper-snaps at me, rocking the sleeping infant in her arms.

I snort. "Quite the mouth in front of your daughter."

She rolls her eyes. "Did Rich tell you?"

I nod. "It's fine. I'm here for Dad and the family, not the bullshit. I just want this to be a good Christmas with everyone. It's what he deserves."

"It's what he *wants*," she corrects me, moving the blanket out of the way so I can take a look at my niece. Her chubby cheeks and long lashes pull at my heartstrings.

"She's beautiful, Nat," I say as Martina comes barreling into the kitchen with my four-year-old nephew, Tucker, hiked up on her shoulders. He looks so much like Natalie, it's pretty amusing. I'd even venture to say I see myself in the little bruiser.

"Uncle MVP," he squeals, bouncing on Martina's shoulders.

Natalie groans as her wife laughs. "I guess he remembered the *cool uncle* nickname you told him to use."

"Hey, Martina," I say, giving her a side hug and swapping her shoulders for mine under Tucker. "How ya doing, kiddo? Your mom told me you're in preschool now."

"Yeah. I have friends." Tucker smiles, gripping my neck.

I chuckle. "Is that so?"

"Dad is in the den...with Eric," my sister tells me, her face turning down in a sour expression. She dislikes him just as much as I do. There's just *something* about the guy that doesn't sit right with us. Sad to say, my parents don't see it.

I lift Tucker off my shoulders and set him down.

"Lunch will be ready shortly," my mother proclaims, coming into the kitchen. "I'm sure you're starving, sweetie. Such a long flight. Leah looks exhausted."

My sister perks up. "They're here? Well, I'd rather see her and that bun in the oven than my brother who never answers my calls." She glares at me as she sashays away, a smile playing on her lips.

Shit.

My mother spins to face me. "You haven't been answering your sister's calls?" She scolds me the only way a mother can. "Nicholas."

I clench my jaw. "Been a busy year, Mom. I'll, uh, be back. I'm going to say hi to Dad."

She waves me off, dismissing me with a clear promise to discuss my 'family priorities' later. I walk through the grand dining room toward the home office. The door is closed and I fight the urge to go in there guns blazing. Schooling my features instead, I push inside.

I'm met with the sight of my father sitting behind his large mahogany desk, and *Eric* sitting in a relaxed pose across from him. It almost looks like they're having a meeting. Almost.

"Nick, my boy," my father bellows, pushing to stand. He looks good, all things considered. He's lost his hair, beard, and eyebrows. He's lost some weight, too, since the last time I saw him, but his color is good, and that little bit I'll hold onto.

"Hey, Dad. How are you?" I ask as I give him a sturdy hug.

"Not too bad, if you'd believe it," he says, sitting back down. "Doctors gave me a break for the holidays. Didn't want me looking like hell for everyone."

My brow furrows. "You sure that's a good idea?"

"You got him the best of the best, didn't you, Nick?" Eric chimes in unwelcomely.

My lip twitches. Prick.

"His insurance did," I sneer, forcing my closed fists into my pockets before my father sees.

"I'm doing well. I've earned the time to take a break and enjoy my family," Dad states, gesturing loosely to the snake in the room. "Eric was just telling me about Darcy. He's looking for some advice about deciding to settle down."

"I'm leaning toward it," Eric says with a chuckle that sounds as forced as him being here. "She's a great girl. Deserves the world, wouldn't you agree, *Nick*?"

Not even close to how I'd describe her. "You'd know."

Eric purses his lips together, turning to face my father. "Well, Darcy's always been big on family, as you know, *Uncle* Bruce."

I narrow my gaze. Wherever he's going with this, I don't like it.

"I was hoping to get Great Grandma Davis' wedding ring for when I inevitably propose." The smirking side eye Eric sends me sets the rage in my chest to a boil.

That good for nothing son of a—

My father appears rather surprised by Eric's request as he turns to me. "Well, that'd be up to Nick here. The ring is passed down to the men in the family." He pauses—too long for my liking. "I...suppose you'd have a right to Grandmother's ring just as much as any other Davis-born son."

Over my dead body.

Before Eric can open his quicksand mouth, I say, "I've met someone."

Dad leans back, raising a brow. "You have? Who?"

Think. Think fast, Nick. "I met her, uh, at the airport."

Eric snorts. "So, what, an hour ago?"

I scowl his way. "No. I met her at the airport last time I came home for a visit. We've been seeing each other for *months*. We're in love and I plan to propose the next time I see her. She's the one, Dad. *I* need Grandma's ring."

Eric crosses his arms, clearly not believing me. Hell, I wouldn't. I've been single for nearly two years, and haven't been on a date in over six months. This is out of left field, even for me.

But he doesn't need to know that.

"What's her name?" Eric presses.

I search my brain for a name—any name—but only one comes to mind. Her stunning smile and airy laugh flood my thoughts, leaving no room for anyone else. "Joy. Joy Bell."

The moment her name rolls off my tongue, a warmth spreads throughout my chest. Whether it's nerves I'll be called out on my clear, boldfaced lie or just the thought of being with my assistant, I couldn't tell you.

"Joy, huh," my father muses. "Why haven't I heard you talk about her?"

"Yeah, *Nick*, why haven't we heard anything about this airport...*fling*?"

It's right then I realize: I've *got* to sell this.

I need this ring.

It's *mine*.

"You'll meet her when she gets here," I announce, pushing the lie home. "She had to do some traveling of her own to see her family before heading this way. I wanted it to be a surprise. You know how Mom is about my dating life. And with the holiday season... I couldn't be answering all of her calls about her future daughter-in-law." I say the words with so much confidence, I can tell, my father is sold.

He leans over, rifling through his top desk drawer. He retrieves a small, velvet box, and stands to slap it in my hand. I quell the urge to ask why the hell he was keeping the ring in his desk and not the safe, when he grips my shoulder. "I completely understand, son. It's yours. Your mother is going to be over the moon with this news. When will she get here?"

Ah, right. *The details.*

"I need to call her and let her know I got in. Her flight was, uh, rescheduled. I'll give her a call now."

Eric stands with a huff. "Yes, well, you better do that. What a romantic proposal it will be in the middle of the airport..."

Dad rumbles a hearty chuckle. "That it will. Proposing in the airport where you two met—we'll be able to have the whole family in attendance for this." He pats me on the back as he moves past me, calling out to my mother with pure joy in his voice. "What a Christmas!"

I stare at the velvet box in my hand. "What a Christmas."

Three.

Joy

What a nightmare.

Not only was my first flight delayed by *three* hours, I missed my connecting flight. Then, I had to wait *six* hours for the next flight. It's been a heck of a trip, but I've finally landed at LAX and I'm itching to see my brother.

It's been too long.

He didn't respond to any of my messages about my crazy travel issues, but it was the middle of the night. So, as I turn my phone off airplane mode, I expect a plethora of return messages from him, but...I don't have any.

Maybe he knew I wouldn't be available while on the plane? *Probably*, I tell myself.

I grab my carry-on and purse and deboard the plane, heading for baggage claim. I try to call my brother twice before he finally answers. "Hello?"

"Hey," I say, breathing a silent sigh of relief. "I finally landed. What a nightmare that was. Where are you? I'm at baggage now."

There's a long pause before Emmett exhales, "Listen, Joy, I've...got to work. A producer is willing to look at my latest project and I can't miss out on an opportunity like this. You understand how it is."

I don't know if it's the overwhelming exhaustion or the fact he's ditching me after I'm already here. "No, Emmett, I don't understand," I practically scream, shocking myself and several people around me with my outburst, their heads whipping in my direction. I take in a deep breath and turn away, speaking in a much calmer, but still agitated tone. "You can't do this to me again. We've had this planned for *months*." When he doesn't respond, I add weakly, "It's Christmas."

"Yeah, I know what time of year it is, sis," he mutters. "I'm sorry, but I have to do this. We'll do Easter on the beach. I promise."

I fight back the tears. He said the same thing last year.

I can't believe I wasted my time and money without hearing from him the last few days. That should've been a sign all on its own. I am an absolute idiot.

"I have to go." I hang up the phone before I say something I'll regret. None of his excuses are going to make me feel better anyhow. This is so typical Emmett Bell. I should've known.

My parents finalized their divorce in the middle of the holidays eight years ago. I had just turned seventeen, while my brother, Emmett, was nineteen at the time. The holidays haven't been the same ever since.

My favorite time of the year simply became chaotic traveling and who-goes-where and who-wants-what. It went from a time of love and family to one of inconvenience and distance.

My father took a job in New York, while my mother stayed in California and remarried within the year to start a new family. It was a shock to the system you could say when she announced she was expecting.

Emmett stayed in California, close to where we grew up so he could pursue his dream of becoming a director, while I headed off to college in Texas for advertising. We've tried our best to remain close since we rarely see each other anymore, but it seems my big brother doesn't have the same family drive as I do.

None of my family does.

Tapping my phone in my hands, I think for a minute. I'm in LA with nowhere to stay four days before Christmas. Hotel prices are ridiculous. Airbnbs are full. I *could* ask Emmett if I can still stay at his place, but I'm so angry with him right now, I know we'd just be fighting the few seconds he bothered to grace me with his presence. It's not even worth it.

There's only one other person I know still in California, though. So I make the call. It takes three rings for my mom to pick up the phone. "Hello?"

"Surprise!" I laugh, feeling delirious from the lack of sleep. "I'm in LA visiting Emmett, and I was wondering—"

"Madison, don't pull your sister's hair," she calls out in the background. "Sorry, what did you say?"

I bite my lip, feeling shockingly uncomfortable talking to my mother for the first time in months. "Um, I'm in town. So, I thought—"

"Oh, you should've called, Joy. Dan and I took the girls to Disney for Christmas. We won't be home until the twenty-ninth."

I could throw up right now. "Oh."

There's a faint commotion on the other end, then crying. "Sorry, hon, I've got to go. I'll talk to you soon, okay? Merry Christmas," she pushes out before the line goes silent.

I lean against a pillar in the middle of baggage claim as the tears fall.

I feel so stupid right now. So, so stupid. Stupid *and* alone for Christmas.

And you know what's even worse? My luggage is nowhere in sight.

⁓⁓⁓

"There has to be something you can do," I say to the desk agent. "My luggage is god knows where, my flights have been either delayed or canceled. I've been stuck here for *hours*. There must be a connecting flight somewhere, anywhere, to get me back to Dallas."

The woman shakes her head, smacking her lips. "Sorry, dear, there's nothing to Dallas until tomorrow night. I can try to find you a hotel, but with the holiday season..."

"Yeah, yeah, I know. Everything is full." I bite my lip as I try to think.

"Hey, lady, are you done?" a man waiting impatiently behind me snaps. "Some of us have planes to catch."

I sigh, utterly defeated. "Right, sorry." I grab my carry-on and move to the side, letting the next person in line go.

I suppose I could just wait... *In the airport overnight?* Even the thought has me cringing.

I need a flight home. Or hot shower and a bed, at the very least.

My phone rings and I quickly fish it out, hoping it's someone calling to tell me a seat opened last minute on an earlier flight—but it's not. It's my boss of all people.

Deep breaths, Joy, deep breaths.

I answer. "Mr. Davis, hi—"

"Joy! Fuck. I've been trying to call you for the last half hour," he pushes out in a single breath. *Did he just use my first name?* "Where are you right now?"

He sounds a little panicked, but I don't want to point that out in case it's just my exhaustion getting to me. "Is everything okay, Mr. Davis?"

"I need you to come to Wisconsin. How soon could you be on a flight to Green Bay?"

"Green Bay?" I'm so confused. "What's wrong, Mr. Davis? Did something happen?"

He inhales deeply on the other end before he says, "Miss Bell, I need you to come to Wisconsin. This is an emergency. I understand it's last minute and you're probably spending time with family right now, but...I need you to get on a flight as soon as possible."

An emergency? "What—"

"*Please.*" There's clear desperation in his voice. If he was trying to hide it before, he isn't now. "I'm begging you. I need you here."

Need. He's used that word one too many times in this very short conversation. I don't think anyone's ever told me they *need* me. A little voice inside my head reminds me that it's Christmas. While another voice says Mr. Davis *is* my boss. It would look good for me to drop everything to come to his aid.

It's also not like I have anything else going on at the moment. *Clearly.*

But he doesn't need to know that.

"Okay," I say, fumbling to find my tablet. "Let me just look up flights to—"

"No need," he says, his tone sounding more than relieved. "I've got everything pulled up online. There's a flight leaving in two hours that connects to Green Bay. I remember you saying you were in LA. Can you get to LAX in the next hour? I'll book this right now while I have you."

I fight back the urge to laugh hysterically. Considering I'm already here, it shouldn't be a problem. "I can."

He types quickly in the background as I relay all my information for him to enter. He emails the confirmation to me and I start walking to the kiosk to print out my *first-class* ticket to Wisconsin.

"I'll be there to pick you up from the airport," he says. "I'll watch the flight tracker, but text me with any delays."

"I will," I say, grabbing my ticket and getting in line to talk to someone about making sure my luggage is rerouted—assuming they ever find it.

"Thank you for doing this." Mr. Davis blows out a breath. "You have no idea what this means to me. Truly."

I smile. "Of course, Mr. Davis."

There's a long pause before he asks, awkwardly, "Are you, uh, seeing anyone right now?"

I freeze. That's an...odd question to ask. "Um, no, I'm not."

"Good," he mumbles before adding, "I'll see you soon...Joy."

He hangs up the phone.

Why the heck is that *good*?

Four.

Nick

I WASN'T ABLE TO convince a single family member to not come with me to the airport to pick up Miss Bell—*Joy*, I remind myself. Shit. I can't be slipping up and calling her *Miss Bell* in front of my family.

I *was*, however, able to convince them to let me drive the rental car alone. While my parents, Natalie, Martina, Tucker, baby Izzy, Rich, Leah, and my Aunt Sara and Uncle Allen—who came in just in time for all the excitement—ride separately in a parade of vehicles.

And by *excitement*, I mean my proposal to a woman I barely know.

We've worked together for the last three months, give or take, and I know nothing personal about her life or who she is outside the office. I've been in my own world since Dad's diagnosis.

My mother tried to have me change into a suit for this, and somehow, I got out of it. Telling her Joy is a *simple woman* and she would rather I be *comfortable*—a complete assumption on my part. I couldn't stop her from insisting I buy flowers to make some sort of 'scene' for when I proclaim my love, though.

I don't know how this spiraled so out of control so damn quickly, because I've got a bouquet of two dozen red roses in my passenger seat and a box of fresh petals to lay at my feet on the spot I'll be proposing to her.

In the middle of the airport.

My phone rings and I hit the Bluetooth connected to my rental to answer, "Hey, Rich. Did you get her HR file?"

Rich is the only one who knows Joy is my assistant and *not* my girlfriend...or soon-to-be fiancée. Well, at least not for real. I had to tell him, and the mortified expression he gave me when I did, has me on edge. He understands *why* I said what I said, but he's just as nervous about how this is going to play out as I am.

"Yeah." My cousin sighs, judgment coming through the speakers. "You sure you want to do this, Nick? I'm sure if you just talk to your dad, he'll understand—"

"No," I bite out. "That's no longer an option. You saw his face. Mom's, too. They need this. And like hell I'm letting fucking Eric take something that belongs to me."

"It's not them I'm worried about," he replies. He's worried about how Joy will respond to this. Me, down on one knee the second I see her, pleading with her to say yes and play along. But it's the only option I have.

"I'll explain everything to her and she'll be compensated for all of her time."

"You could've told her over the phone before you bought the plane ticket," he mutters. "Give the poor woman a chance to know what she's about to walk into."

I thought about that, but I didn't want to give her the chance to say no, that she wasn't coming. Especially after she told me she would come at a last second's notice. I'll have to ask her how the hell she swung that and make sure she's reimbursed accordingly.

"Read me what you have in her file," I tell him. I need to know everything I can before I get to this airport. It's the bare minimum, but it'll have to do.

Rich says something to Leah, instructing her to read off the attached file in his email. I knew Leah would find out eventually. Rich isn't one to keep secrets from her, rightfully so.

The less people who know this one, though, the better.

"Joy Mara Bell. She's twenty-five years old. She went to the University of Houston for her bachelors in advertising and moved to Dallas two years ago. She worked with a few agencies before landing at Davis Sporting Goods as a promotions assistant. She has a clean record and an amazing credit score." Leah trails off quietly, "How is she so young with a credit score like this, honey?"

"She probably—"

"Guys, focus," I snap. We're less than five minutes from the airport, we can't be having these side conversations. "What else?"

"Um..." There's a long pause. "That's really it. She lived in Los Angeles most of her life and moved to Dallas after college. There's not much here."

Shit. "All right. Thanks, Rich."

"Hey, uh, Nick," Leah starts, "have you thought about what could happen if she says no?"

My chest feels tight at the thought alone.

I've been intentionally avoiding the very *idea* she might tell me no.

The plan is, if I can keep a good distance between myself and my family during this proposal, I should be able to convince her to play along. I'll have to do a lot of pleading with my eyes, subtle cues. Let's just hope she picks up on them.

"Just...keep everyone back so they can't hear what I say to her, all right?"

When our parade of vehicles arrives at the airport, everyone heads inside. Her flight took off a few minutes late, but it looks like they'll be arriving on time. My mother takes charge, mapping out the small area at baggage claim to get a *lay of the land*. Thankfully, she also wants everyone to give me a private moment with Joy before she's bombarded by meeting the family for the first time.

I pick a spot and call it good. I lay out the rose petals at my mother's instruction—my father looking on with amusement and a beaming smile.

I'll take that smile, I decide. If I go through all this ending in Miss Bell suing me for harassment, at least my parents are thrilled.

Everyone moves back, and my sister gives me a suspicious side-eye. She wasn't as easily convinced as my parents were six hours ago, and either she's choosing to let them have this, same as me, or she's waiting to get me cornered for questioning.

I ignore the dozens of prying eyes between passing travelers and take out my phone to check she's landed. Another few minutes and she'll be coming this way.

My palms start to sweat holding this cliché bouquet. My knees are locked with an anxious twitch, ready to buckle and drop down to one knee the moment I see her.

Should I wait to kneel? Try and whisper to her about the situation? Or go in full throttle?

She has no idea what she's walking into...

I've got this, I tell myself. *I can sell this to her.*

Sell it to her so she'll sell it to my entire family.

Fuck.

It's not another five minutes before I spot her. I see her long before she sees me and I take the moment to look her over. She's got a large bag slung over her shoulder and a carry-on wheeling at her side. I recognize her clothing as the DSG women's yoga apparel. High-waisted, lavender yoga pants, and a light-grey cropped hoodie paired with white sneakers.

She's stunning. I always found her appealing to look at, her body a perfect hourglass shape with full curves. But...looking at her now outside of the office, dressed how she is, with my mind focused solely on *her* and what I'm about to do...I realize how beautiful she truly is.

From her thighs to the pop of her hips and plump ass, the dip of her waist as it curves out to her ample breasts. All the way up to her lush lips and hazel eyes. Her long, dark hair is slung up high in a ponytail, swinging from side to side as she walks this way.

And the closer she gets, the harder my heart hammers in my chest.

I didn't even think about her coming from sunny California to below-freezing Wisconsin. She went from perfect beach weather to several feet of snow. I'll have to figure out an excuse, a reason for why she didn't come weather appropriate.

She peers around for a second and, as the crowd clears a path to baggage, she sees me.

The smile she sends my way is...gorgeous. And it fades faster than I hoped it would as she takes in the sight of me.

Here goes nothing.

Joy

I STARE AHEAD AS I make my slow, cautious way over to Mr. Davis.

He's standing in the middle of baggage claim in a poorly shaped heart made of rose petals while holding a massive bouquet of red roses.

My mind is struggling to grasp what's going on.

If I didn't know any better, I'd say it looks like he's ready to propose to someone. Only, as far as I know, based on the office gossip courtesy of Lisa, Mr. Davis is a bachelor. He's been single for the last few years—something about a messy breakup caused by a distant family member.

So, what's he doing? Does he have a secret relationship? Is that why he called me here, to help him plan his proposal?

It's the only plausible explanation.

Well, if this is his setup, it's not bad. Rather romantic, I think. Picking up your sweetheart from the airport and proposing to them on the spot? I'd take that.

Although, he could've worn something a little nicer for the occasion.

He's dressed in a heavy, outdoor coat with a black hoodie underneath and dark wash jeans paired with winter boots. I've never seen him so casual, so...out of the office. His thick chestnut hair is a little disheveled and I notice there's a beanie half-stuffed in his pocket. He hasn't appeared to have shaved since the last time I saw him at the company Christmas party, letting a dusting of facial hair grow over his strong jaw the last day or so. It's a good look on him.

I bob and weave around the clusters of people, and go right to him. I put on a smile to try and mask how tired and *ridiculously* cold I am given we're indoors.

"Hi, how are—"

Mr. Davis doesn't give me a chance to finish before he's wrapping a strong arm around my waist. He pulls me in, nearly crushing the beautiful bouquet between us. I gasp as our bodies touch in such a way that feels highly inappropriate and deliciously hot all at once.

"I'll explain everything, I swear," he whispers deeply in my ear, his breathing rapid alongside his hushed words. "Play along."

Huh? Play along with what?

He takes the smallest step back, pushing the bouquet of roses into my fumbling hands.

I'm so confused. I must have misheard that last part. "What are you—"

I gasp as Mr. Davis drops down to one knee right in front of me.

He clears his throat and digs in his jacket pocket before pulling out that signature, black velvet ring box most women hope to see one day.

I watch in disbelief as he opens the box, revealing a rose gold, diamond engagement ring that looks so delicate, so stunning, it steals the breath from my lungs. Another small gasp slips out of me as I hug the bouquet to my chest. I've never seen anything like it. Wherever he got this ring, it's clearly one of a kind.

Dark chocolate eyes, molten with clear determination in this moment—and nerves—hold my gaze. I've never seen Mr. Davis this nervous before. The next words out of his mouth, however, nearly knock me over, "Joy Mara Bell, will you do me the honor of becoming my wife? Will you marry me?"

My eyes widen and I feel every muscle in my body tense. I'm so dang flabbergasted, all I can do is stare at him. *What* did he just say? Marry *him*?

How does he know my middle name?

"Say yes," he whispers, nearly hissing the words under his breath.

What is going on? "Mr. Da—"

"Say. *Yes*," he hisses again, his face heating. There's desperation in the way he's gazing up at me from his vulnerable position—down on one knee in the middle of baggage claim with dozens of travelers stopped to watch a seemingly romantic proposal.

My throat struggles to work.

He's serious.

No, correction: He is *dead* serious.

Play along, he said. But I can't form words right now, so all I do is nod vigorously. My body is shaking from the shock—of whatever this is—and the fact it feels like I'm about to cry. This is probably the last thing he wants to see, but I don't think I can stop the floodgates on this one.

No one's ever proposed to me before.

Is it lame if I get choked up at the mere premise of being proposed to? Maybe, but if this is a *play-it-out* situation, I would hope the lucky lady who ends up on the other end of this proposal sheds a few tears as well.

Mr. Davis beams as he gets to his feet. He wraps me in his strong embrace and plucks me off my feet. I instinctively throw my arms around his neck as he holds me against him.

Several people begin clapping and cheering around us.

The tears fall as I choke out a quiet sob, squeezing my boss around his neck. *My boss*. I must be delirious from the lack of sleep I've gotten over the last two days, because I swear, he holds me back just as tight. His arms should *not* feel this good. His embrace is like a warm, cozy blanket that I want to cocoon myself in and never come out of.

When he sets me back on my feet, I pull away with a sniffle. "Sorry," I whisper, barely audible as I quickly wipe my wet cheeks and try to fix the crushed roses in the bouquet. I feel so...embarrassed. Who cries at a fake proposal?

The last ten hours of my life have been complete chaos. I came here to help my boss with an emergency, not get all gushy over his practice proposal.

Mr. Davis leans down, his arms still around my waist. "Don't be." He brushes the dampness from my cheeks with his thumb. "You're doing great, Joy. I'll explain everything when we're alone."

I don't get a chance to register his words before he takes my left hand in his. My heart nearly stops as he removes the engagement ring from the box and slips it onto my ring finger.

This ring is too darn gorgeous and fits too darn good for me to be even *attempting* to think straight. I choke back another sob. I'm too emotional for this.

"Why—" I'm dazed, my mind a muddled mess as he leans down and kisses my forehead.

I can't even remember what I was about to ask him.

"You're my fiancée, remember that," he says against my flushed skin. "And call me Nick," he adds while tucking me under his arm and turning us toward a group of people coming this way.

"Did she say yes?" An older man chuckles, earning a collective laugh from the group.

Before I know it, I'm promptly thrown into a whirlwind of introductions as Nick Davis' fiancée.

Six.

Nick

I STAY AS CLOSE to Joy's side as my family will allow. She's swallowed by the arms of every family member who tagged along to watch my proposal today.

Fake proposal, mind you.

I realized about five seconds after Joy started crying how asinine this whole idea of mine is. Rich was right. I should've prepared her for what she was walking into.

Until I remember her reaction, and how genuine it was. Her little gasps, her excited—albeit shocked—expression, the way she clutched the bouquet to her chest, to the tears that followed. If I didn't already know that was a sham proposal, I'd say that went pretty damn well.

Any suspicions my sister had are long gone, Rich is stunned into silence at how smoothly that just went, and Leah is torn with what I'm doing.

My mother pulls Joy in for another lung-crushing hug before holding her at arm's length and giving her a once-over. "Oh, you're absolutely gorgeous, dear. My new daughter. Simply perfect, isn't she, Bruce?"

My father grins. "You said it, sweetheart. Welcome to the family, Joy."

Joy's eyes grow suspiciously glossy as she peers up at me beside her. My chest feels tight not knowing if she's mad or upset or planning to find a lawyer in the next five minutes. I don't like seeing her cry. I've never seen her cry, actually, but I don't like it.

And I certainly don't enjoy knowing I'm the reason for it.

My mother starts to scold my father, "Look what you did, Bruce, you made the poor thing cry again."

Joy waves them off, accepting a tissue my aunt hands her. "No, no. It's so nice to meet all of you. I just...had a long flight."

I clear my throat, gently tugging her to me and away from my family. She fits perfectly under my arm, and I can't deny the spike of pleasure I have when she leans into me.

"All right, all right, let her breathe," I say, leaning down to lay a kiss on her temple. Overdoing it? Perhaps, but I did tell myself I *had* to sell this. "How many bags did you bring, babe?"

Her sharp intake of breath is quiet enough I'm confident I'm the only one who hears it. Yet, it makes me nervous all the same.

Too much? Should I dial it back? Was it the second kiss or the endearment?

"Oh, um, one, but...it got lost from Dallas to LA." She looks up at me wearily. "It's been a rough day," she confesses.

Before I can respond, my father is taking charge of the situation. Anytime there's an issue to be solved, he's the first one in line to fix it. So it's no surprise he's already on it. "Don't worry, dear, we'll see what we can find out," he announces, waving for Uncle Al to follow him to the recovery office near baggage.

Tucker and Martina start to clean up the scattered rose petals. "When I proposed to Natalie, we saved the petals and used them on our wedding day at the altar." She gives me a coy smile. "It's good luck to save the petals from the most monumental moments in our lives. At least, that's what my abuela taught me."

Joy's smile is infectious. "That's beautiful."

"Hold on, honey," my sister says, adjusting Izzy in her arm with her phone in hand. She gestures between Joy and me. "I got the whole thing on video, but I want a few pictures. Quick. Get together before Tuck gets all the petals."

I chuckle, watching my nephew's fast hands while using his shirt as a makeshift basket. "I think it's a little late for that, Nat."

She huffs at me. "Do it anyway. You'll want the extra photos. Trust me."

Martina snatches Tucker and Joy's carry-on from the frame. A second later, my mother and Aunt have their phones out as well, aimed at the newly engaged couple—*us.*

Joy shifts to hug me around my waist, smiling for the camera with her face pressed to the side of my chest. My pulse picks up at the way she's clinging to me. I grin down at her as I follow her lead, sliding my arm over the small of her back and pressing her deeper against me.

"Aw, that's cute, Nick," my sister beams. "Joy, look up at Nick quick."

Following my sister's instruction, Joy gazes up at me. Her smile turns into a sweet laugh that has my smile growing. Several pictures are captured before we call it good. The petals are collected as my father and uncle return with bad news about Joy's luggage still being MIA.

"'Tis the season." Aunt Sara shakes her head. "Luggage thieves are a real thing, and the busiest time of the year is the easiest target. I'd imagine LA is full of them."

My family starts a debate if that's really what happened to the missing luggage or not. I, however, am ready to get the hell out of here, get my assistant alone, and beg her to stay through the week.

I glance at Joy's small carry-on. "We'll stop to grab a few things before heading to the house."

My father nods sternly, laying a firm hand on my shoulder. "Absolutely, son. The women in our lives always come first, am I right?" He winks.

My mother squeezes in, giving myself and Joy a hug. "We'll see you soon, dears. Love you both!"

The group shuffles toward the exit. I gently urge my *fiancée* to follow, but she seems rooted in place, her eyes glossy...again. I set my jaw, needing to contain my impatience. "Let's go."

Her shallow nod seems to release her legs at my nudge, guiding her forward. When we get to the door, though, I catch the strong shiver she lets out before hugging herself.

Right. LA to North Tree.

I take off my coat. "Here. Put this on."

She mutely slips her arms in. I help her zip it and tug the hood over her head. I pull my hat on and grab her carry-on while keeping a hand on her lower back to guide her to the car. It's not another few minutes before we're finally alone and I'm cranking up the heat for us both.

I wait a beat to see if she'll say something first, but she just stares ahead at my parents loading in their truck with Tucker.

Where do I start? "I need you to stay with me throughout the week as my fiancée." There, that about sums it up.

She glances at me out of the corner of her eye, her makeup lightly smeared. "You *need* me to stay. Are you asking me or telling me, Mr. Davis?"

I fight back a wince at her tone. I'm getting the sense reality is sinking in for her and she may be a little...frustrated with me. *Yeah, frustrated, we'll go with that.* "Uh, both?"

Her snort of laughter is sarcastic. She drags a hand down the side of her face. "How about you tell me what's going on, *Nick*? Then

I'll decide if I shouldn't run back into that airport and wait for the next available flight to Dallas."

"You'd be waiting until tomorrow night if you did," I grumble.

The look she gives me is incredulous.

I sigh, rubbing my bristled chin. "My father's always been a big family man—family comes first, and all that. My Uncle Steve was, too. They started Davis Sporting Goods together back in the 80s. Four years ago, my uncle died in a car accident." I pause, shaking my head. "They always said DSG would be run by family and family alone, but my uncle had no biological children that my father was aware of, so the business fell to myself and my sister. Natalie was more interested in law school, so the family business fell on me."

"And Mr. Hanes—Rich, is your...cousin?"

"My mother's nephew." I nod. "Anyway, about two years ago, *Eric Davis* showed up. The long-lost bastard son of my late uncle. It was a shock to the family, to say the least. I mean, he just appeared out of thin air, demanding he get his cut of his late father's legacy—out of Davis Sporting Goods."

Joy's brow furrows, tipping her head. "That's a little...odd."

I throw my hands in the air. "Exactly. Why my parents can't see that, is beyond me. They welcomed him with open arms. It's been a battle trying to get him to do anything related to actually working for the company. All he wants is *money*. He's a snake, Joy, and he's taken too much from this family already. I won't allow him to take what's rightfully mine. I won't."

She nods slowly, processing my outburst for all it's worth.

I stare at the ring on her finger and my chest tightens. "That ring was my great grandmother's," I say as she follows my line of sight. "My father always told me he wanted the ring to be handed down to the Davis son who found love first. To continue the tradition started with my great grandfather. At the time, my uncle had no sons, so the ring was going to be mine no matter what."

"He wanted the ring?" she asks, putting the pieces together.

"When I got here this morning, I found him in my father's office, asking for the ring for a proposal he never intends on making. I couldn't let him take the ring, Joy. I knew if he got his grimy hands on it, not only would I never see it again, but it wouldn't stay in the family like my father wishes." I sigh, fighting the words out, "I did the only thing I could think of... I told my father that I needed the ring because I intended to propose today as a surprise for them and...you."

"*Me?*"

"You're the only one I could think of at the time." I don't mention how, looking back, I wouldn't choose anyone other than her. For this, that is.

The deep intake of breath she makes has my nerves breaking. I need her to go along with this. I need it. My family needs it. This has to work. At least for the week. "You'll be compensated for your time however you see fit," I say. "Within reason, of course."

She raises a brow. "You want to pay me to lie to your family?"

"Yes." To put it simply. "Rich is already drawing up something for you to sign. I can make a partial transfer by tomorrow morning into your account."

She shakes her head. "I'm not a good liar, Mr. Davis."

"Nick," I correct her. "And that's fine. You don't have to lie...directly. I just need you to play my fiancée and stay at my parents' house for the rest of the week."

Her head falls back against the headrest, and she slips down into the extra depths of my oversized coat wrapped around her. Her brows are knitted together as she gnaws on her lush lower lip before her gaze drifts to me.

She's going to say no. I can feel it.

"My father is sick, as I'm sure you noticed," I say, playing the only card I have left. And a solid, pity card it is. "Pancreatic cancer, stage four. The doctors gave him a year to live." I swallow hard remembering the pain I felt when I first heard the news. "That was six months ago. He's responded well enough to treatment to buy him some time, but that doesn't mean this won't be his last Christmas with us."

Her expression softens. "I'm so sorry."

I rub the back of my neck. "It's been a lot," I confess. "I'm sorry I dragged you here, Joy. I wasn't thinking straight earlier. I understand if you can't stay." It's true, now that I say it. There's been too much clouding my judgment lately. I've taken it out on the people closest to me and I'm suddenly ashamed I even thought up this ridiculous master plan to save my grandmother's ring.

The silence between us is long and heavy as I wait for her decision. I half expect her to demand I book her a hotel and flight back to Dallas before we leave this parking lot.

Sitting up, she turns to me. "I'll stay."

My heart leaps in my chest. I straighten, fighting down a grin as I tug my phone from my pocket. "I'll call Rich right now and—"

She puts her hand up, stopping me short. "I don't want your money."

My brow furrows. "Are you sure? I don't want you to think this is part of your job. I realize I'm keeping you from spending time with your family for Christmas."

She winces at my words. It's subtle, but it's there. "I'm sure," she says, adding with a glance outside, "Although, I could use a winter coat and pair of boots if I'll be staying for the week."

I grin despite myself, pulling the car out of park. "I know just the place."

Seven.

Joy

"THIS IS THE FIRST ever Davis Sporting Goods," *Nick* tells me as he parks outside in the snow-covered lot. The building is smaller than the grand, spacious stores I've been to, and it doesn't quite match the fresh, clean-cut atmosphere of the brand now. There's something...different about this store. It's warmer, welcoming.

I climb out to head inside, huddling into my boss' coat that smells like crisp winter air and warm cedar. I inhale deeply. No man's coat has *any* business smelling this dang delicious.

Trudging through the snow, Nick walks beside me, trying to block the icy wind. He's chivalrous, I'll give him that.

He just wants you to 'play along' like a good little assistant. I frown at the thought.

He gave me the opportunity to say no twice now. His plan is…insane, honestly, but I understand why he's doing it. I'd do the same, wouldn't I? There are some things you just can't let slide.

Like your brother ditching you for Christmas.

Or an estranged relative coming in and demanding their dues.

It's off-putting, the idea of lying to his family. They've already welcomed me with such kind, open arms, and with his father's health status… The least I can do is be here for him and his family. Even if that means pretending to be someone I'm not. And if we're being truthful with ourselves, the thought of enjoying Christmas as a family—even if it's not my own—is more than enough compensation.

A quaint bell above the door chimes as we walk inside. The interior matches the exterior: original and wholesome. "Welcome to Davis Sporting Goods," an older gentleman announces as the door closes behind us with a bitter whistle from the wind.

Nick smiles at the sight of the man behind the register. "Hello, Jerry. How's business?"

The man lifts his gaze and beams. "Nick!" he hoots, shuffling around the counter and engulfing him in a sure embrace. "What a pleasant surprise seeing you here. How's the family?"

"Everyone's well, Jer," he replies. "And yours?"

"Good, good." Jerry's gaze slides to me. "And who might this pretty young lady be? What are you doing walking around with this overworked lug?" He chuckles.

Nick's arm circles my waist as I extend a hand, adding, "I'm Joy. Nick's fiancée." The words taste funny on my tongue even as my chest heats and my stomach flip-flops.

My announced fiancé tugs me closer.

"My, my. Congratulations, you two." He whistles. "Meredith is going to be scuffed she missed you both."

"We'll see you both on Tuesday, won't we?" Nick asks.

"Of course." Jerry nods. "We wouldn't miss a traditional Davis Christmas Eve for the world," he says, gesturing between us. "Now, what can I help you lovebirds find this evening? Ice skates for tomorrow, I assume?"

There's ice skating?

"Not today," Nick says. "We lost some of the missus' luggage, so we need a pair of boots and a suitable coat for this weather we're having."

"Ah." Jerry waves us to follow. "We don't have much left in stock, but I'm sure you'll find something. Doesn't need to be pretty, right?" He laughs. "The snow just keeps coming, I'm telling you." He leads us to the winter coats, pointing out which racks are on sale before making a joke they'll be *on the house* when the front door chimes with another customer. "Holler if you kids need anything. Boots are along the far wall."

A moment later, we're alone for the third time in the last twenty-four hours—or has it been less than that? I don't know. Time feels like an illusion at the current moment.

I snort to myself, flipping through the fluffy hoods.

"For someone who claims to not be good at lying, I'd say that went rather smoothly," Nick says quietly, pushing his hands in his jeans' pockets.

I give him a subtle side-eye. "Was that a test, *honey*?"

He grins, shrugging. "If it was, you passed with flying sleigh bells."

I laugh, plucking a long down coat from the rack for closer inspection. "So, should we do a little...preliminary prep for this week?"

"Like what?"

"Well, you don't know much about me," I say, shimmying off his jacket and handing it to him. "I mean, I'd like to think I know the basics about you."

He folds it over his forearm, eyeing me. "Really now. And what would that be?"

I proceed to rattle off his entire work schedule, favorite breakfast, lunch, and dinner spots, workout routine, how he hates an *under*-toasted bagel, his birthday, that he's thirty-five, his blood type, all the way down to his regular bathroom breaks—all of which causes his face to flame a cute shade of pink.

"Point taken," he mutters.

I shrug, batting my lashes. "I know my boss."

He crosses his arms, eyeing me as I try the coat on for size and promptly place it back for a different color. "It seems I called the right woman for the job then," he says.

I'm not necessarily looking for his praise, but…it is nice to be acknowledged for being good at something. "I'm, um, glad you did," I add, trying on the deep red version of the lengthy coat that falls below my knees. I check myself out in the mirror and do a turn to the left and right before glancing at Nick. "What do you think?"

He looks me over from head to toe. He takes one long stride toward me and reaches to tug the faux fur-lined hood up. The rough backs of his hands graze over my jaw and my body temperature rises ten degrees.

Could be the coat? Could be the man? We may never know.

The fuzzy, multi-brown shaded fur tickles my cheeks as I tilt my head to peer up at him. He's gazing down at me with a crooked grin and a glint in his eye. "I think you look…" he hesitates, his grin faltering, "…warm."

I push down the disappointed feeling that overcomes me at his choice of adjective.

This isn't a whimsical Christmas love story, Joy, control yourself.

I decide on the coat and we head toward the boots. "So, what should I know about you, then?" he asks as I hunt for my size in a sea of boxes. "Say…things I wouldn't know from your HR file."

I spin on him. "You pulled my HR file? When?"

He makes a face that screams *caught*. "A few hours ago."

Before he knew I'd say yes? "That was awfully presumptuous of you."

"I was hopeful," he says, adding with a smirk, "So, what's on the cheat sheet for getting to know the future Mrs. Joy Davis?"

He's joking. He's *joking.*

Damn him and that perfect cheeky grin.

I control my racing thoughts by considering what information could come up this week that may put us in a corner. I decide to tell him the equivalent of what I know about him: my favorite restaurants, how I take my tea since I don't drink coffee, my top five reality TV shows, and a basic rundown of my daily routine outside of working for him. I opt *not* to go into detail about my depressing family dynamics.

"Oh, and I'm allergic to penicillin," I tell him.

"Penicillin. Got it." He nods.

We walk toward the front with my new boots and coat in hand. "Did you kids find everything you need?" Jerry asks when we reach the register.

"We did," Nick replies as he removes the security tags from the items. I tug on my new gear when Nick grabs a rusty orange knit hat with a matching pompom on the top and hands it to me. "This too, Jer."

I take my hair down and quickly pull the hat over my head. I'm warm from head to toe and I can't help smiling at him. "Good call...*babe.*" I try out the pet name for fun, and to gauge his reaction.

The rugged, handsome grin he sends my way feels like a gift in itself.

Joy

AFTER STOPPING AT ANOTHER local store before heading to the house, we're finally pulling into Nick's parents' long drive.

"This is beautiful," I can't help but comment. I lean forward to stare at the grand, log cabin home decorated in classic holiday lights and décor. It's a winter wonderland covered in several feet of pristine, untouched snow.

"Mom goes all out," Nick mutters.

He kills the engine but makes no show of moving even as I reach for the door.

"Last chance to bail out," he offers, glancing at me. "Once we step through those doors, you're mine for the week," he says with a husky undertone that has my pulse fluttering.

I smile through the flutters. "Well, when you say it like that... How can I refuse?" *Stop flirting*, I mentally scold. *You need to work with this man after all is said and done.*

He grins, pushing open the door with his boot and jogging around the car to my side. He opens my door and takes my hand in his. He grabs my carry-on and keeps me close as we walk toward the front door.

We're a breath away from entering when I give his hand a light squeeze.

He stops as I shift on my feet. "Nervous?"

I peer up at him. "A little," I confess.

"Me, too." He leans in, adding quietly, "We're in this together, okay? I won't leave you to the wolves."

"I thought the expression was *throw* to the wolves," I whisper in return, fighting a smile.

"That, too." He smirks, turning the handle, and pushing us inside.

The house is a bustle of activity. The scent of freshly baked gingerbread floods my senses and I breathe in the strong, cinnamon-laced air as the boisterous sound of laughter greets my ears. Warmth spreads throughout my chest. It's been so long since I've felt this much...holiday spirit.

I can *feel* it growing the more I process what this next week is going to entail.

And I'd be lying if I said I wasn't starting to get excited.

We remove our coats and hang them by the door, kicking off our damp boots as well. When I reach for my things, Nick stops me. "We'll take it up later," he says. "They're probably waiting on us to eat."

"Oh." My hand falls to my side and I bite the inside of my cheek, glancing around the entryway. "Should we…"

"Nicky!"

His jaw tightens.

I peer past him as he greets, "Darcy." His tone is cold as I take in the sight of the perky blonde he doesn't seem too pleased to see. She prances over in a sparkly, beige knit sweater dress and tights, throwing herself at my fake fiancé as if he's her *real* fiancé.

The sight causes a pang of jealousy to heat my blood, surprising me.

I'm not the jealous type…usually.

She clings to him even as he keeps his arms at his sides, confirming to me this isn't a friendly encounter. He mentioned his long-lost cousin dating someone. Is this her?

Blonde hair whips me in the face once she finally releases Nick from his apparent torture. Her gaze lands on me and I decide to step closer to Nick, sliding my hand into his with a tangle of our fingers.

"I heard you were bringing someone," she muses. "I just didn't have the heart to believe it." She extends her hand to me, eyeing me in a way that, from woman to woman, I can tell she isn't happy I'm here—or with Nick. "I'm Darcy."

I shake her hand. "Joy. Nick's fiancée."

A blind man wouldn't miss the twitch in Darcy's eye as she stares down at Nick's great grandmother's ring sitting on my left hand. "It would appear so," she says before her attention shifts to Nick, her voice bouncing with her words. "Congratulations on your...sudden engagement."

My brow furrows. Why would she say it like that?

"Well, you know what they say," Nick chimes, his arm circling my waist as he tugs me against him. "When you know, you know. Right, darling?"

He gazes down at me and reaches out to tilt my face upward. His lips gravitate toward mine. His breath ghosts over my lips as he slides his tongue over the seam of them, asking for permission. I grant it and place a hand between his collar and jaw to hold me steady. The moment is almost enough to drown out the retreat of Darcy's sparkly heels against the hardwoods.

Nick, however, doesn't notice. He pulls me in, deepening the kiss. And it takes everything in me to draw back. His gaze is heated as I do—until he looks over his shoulder and realizes we're alone.

He takes a step back. "Sorry, I—"

"It's fine," I murmur, taking his hand in mine. His gaze darkens and he grips my hand firmly as I say, "Lead the way, fiancé."

We enter the dining room hand in hand and the space lights up with a warm welcome even at our late arrival. The grand table is set for fifteen in a more classic Christmas feel than the exterior. My head is on a swivel admiring it all. Growing up, my mother would decorate, of course, but never like this. *This* is on a whole other level.

Nick subtly reintroduces me to everyone I met at the airport mere hours ago, including a few new faces. His grandparents on his mother's side, Frank and Ethel, and his cousin—the snake in the grass, Nick mentioned—Eric.

"Sorry we missed the action," his cousin says, Darcy at his side as he shakes my hand a bit longer than I'm comfortable with. "It's great to finally meet you."

"You, too." I smile.

Eric releases his hold only to continue staring at me. He's maybe four or five inches taller than me—nothing compared to Nick's towering stature—and yet, I get the impression he's *trying* to make me feel small. As if I'm beneath him. Unwelcome, even.

I don't like it.

By all accounts he looks harmless with his shaggy, light brown hair, wearing casual slacks and a button-down shirt. *Lipstick on a polar bear*, as my father would call it. Nick is wrung taut beside me, and I can see why. There's something...off about him. I make a mental note to ask more questions later when we're alone.

Eric takes his seat next to Darcy, who hasn't spoken another word to us, and Nick leads me around the table to our seats.

"Sit, sit," Mrs. Davis calls, carrying a large dish to the table. She places it down amongst a sea of others. Every signature dish you'd see during the holidays is spread out before us. "You're just in time."

With Nick's father at the head of the table—and Eric at the other—we're seated in the middle beside Rich and Leah. Nick's sister, Natalie, and her little family across from us. I peer over at my *fiancé* only to find him glaring at the far end of the table. I touch his knee to get his attention and his head snaps to me.

"I don't think your mom would be very happy if your cousin spontaneously combusted in the middle of dinner," I whisper-tease.

The tightness in his shoulders visibly eases as a soft smile graces his lips. "She'd forgive me."

I smile, passing the green beans to him when they come around. Conversations float around the table filled with smiles and laughter. The night seems to be going well, considering how tense Nick's been this entire time. I decide to make it my mission that he has fun this week. Why waste energy on some jerk when you could be eating pumpkin pie with extra whipped cream or brownies cut in the shape of Christmas trees with green frosting and sprinkles?

"Oh, not those, dear," Mrs. Davis says, plucking the red Santa container from my hands before I can take it out to the dining room for dessert. She returns them to their spot in the fridge. "Those are Bruce's *special* brownies." She winks.

My brow furrows as Aunt Sara shuffles in with a chuckle. "They're drugged!" she hoots with laughter and Mrs. Davis rolls her eyes, smiling.

"They're baked with marijuana," Mrs. Davis tells me. "He's never been a big fan of smoking, you know, and his doctor recommended it to help manage his stress and to help him relax more. They also help him sleep after those god-awful treatments."

"Oh," I breathe, a pang in my chest at the reminder of Nick's father's declining health. "I, um, I'm so sorry. When Nick told me—"

She pats my shoulder. "No need to be sorry, dear. It's no one's fault." Her eyes shimmer in the warm lighting of the awe-inspiring kitchen any chef, baker, or mac & cheese maker would die to cook in. "We're over the moon to see our son find love during such a hard time. I haven't seen him this happy in years."

Do not *cry, Joy.* "That's...really sweet of you to say, Mrs. Davis," I push out. "And thank you for inviting me into your home. It's breathtaking. I can't imagine how long it took you to decorate all of this."

"You're too kind, Joy," she beams, pulling me in for a hug—the second one this evening and the fourth one today. "And please, call me Betty. Bruce, too. He'll have a field day if he hears you using Mr. and Mrs. Davis." She chuckles, handing me a green Christmas tree container filled with 'family friendly' brownies.

I walk the treats out to the dining room with a smile on my face—only to realize Nick is talking about...me.

"She's in advertising," he announces, leaving out the part where I work for DSG, or that I'm also his personal assistant.

"Whereabouts?" Bruce asks. "We're always looking for better eyes at Davis."

My smile becomes pained as I open the container and set it on the table. Tucker dives for one immediately, stuffing it into his face before Natalie can catch him.

"What's the name of that place again, Joy?" Nick asks me, a nervous jump in his leg as I sit back down.

"A temp agency," I lie cooly, surprising myself. "Nowhere anyone here has heard of, honey."

Betty shuffles in with yet another pie. "Well, it sounds like you'll be a perfect fit in the family business, Joy-dear," she adds, glancing at the head of the table.

"I'm not sure if Nick mentioned," his father says, "but it's always been the goal for the whole family to grow together as a unit. It's one of the reasons Steve and I started Davis Sporting Goods to begin with." He starts to get a bit emotional at the very mention of his late brother. "We wanted something to live on for generations. Something to sustain our families and so on."

"That's beautiful," I can't help but say aloud, blushing as Darcy and Eric laugh (hopefully not at me) at the other end of the table. Because for Bruce and his brother to think of future generations as a growing unit, for him to put his family—his *family's* families—first, is just... I'm speechless.

Uncle Allen raises his glass of amber liquid. "Hear, hear!"

Nick's arm slides around my waist, his sure hand resting firmly over my hip and thigh—*grazing* my butt. I peer up at him and lose all train of thought as he grins from ear to ear. Why is he so smiley? Was it something I said?

"To family," he says, his gaze on me as he raises his glass to clink his uncle's.

Bruce begins to tell the long-winded origin story of his sporting goods empire. Dessert finishes and I help Betty and Aunt Sara clear the table. I'm in the kitchen loading the dishwasher when my jaw cracks with a massive yawn. Between all the craziness of getting 'engaged' upon arrival, I've forgotten that it's been a long, *long* day.

"Ready to head up?" said fiancé asks behind me as I close the door to the dishwasher.

I turn, finding him on the other side of the central, six-seater island. "Ready if you are," I say, then promptly cover my mouth with another yawn.

He grins. "Rich and Leah are staying in the guest house, so, uh, we'll be in my room. If that's all right with you."

I nod, my cheeks heating at the very thought of sharing a space with him—let alone a *bed*. The feeling is short-lived, however, from the pure exhaustion that washes over me. Do I really care? I'm so tired I'll be asleep the second my head hits the pillow, I'm sure of it.

We say our goodnights to the few still lingering around the dining room, noting the disappearance of his cousin and girlfriend. "Is everyone staying here at the house?" I ask as we gather my things from the foyer.

"Not everyone," he says, hefting my carry-on while I grab my purse. "My grandparents live right up the road, but they'll be here every day this week. Eric and Darcy got a hotel as far as I know. So, yeah, everyone else will be up first thing in the morning. Wouldn't be surprised if we hear Izzy crying at some point tonight."

I yawn, following him up the stairs to his bedroom. "I'm sure it'll be fine."

We make a left at the top of the staircase and walk to the end of the hall before he opens a door on the right. I take in the space, noting the dark wood finishes and the large king-size bed with a four-poster bedframe that takes up a majority of the room. There are two more doors on either side of the room, one is open revealing an ensuite bathroom and I can only assume the other is a closet.

"Did you want to use the bathroom first?" he asks, closing the door behind us. He rolls my bag toward the unopened door to a *massive* walk-in closet.

I would've *killed* for a closet like that growing up.

"This is your room," I say, then realize how *duh* it sounds. Shaking my head with a laugh, I set my purse on the nightstand furthest from the door on instinct. "I mean, was this your childhood bedroom?"

"Mine? No." He chuckles. "My sister and I shared a bedroom until I was eight. That's about when DSG started taking off. We upgraded to a three-bedroom in town, that's where my parents lived for about fifteen years before building this house. Their *dream family gathering home* as my mother loves to call it."

I smile. "Your family is amazing."

Nick leans a shoulder against the door frame to the closet. "You did pretty amazing yourself down there."

"I've been known to tell a white lie or two." I shrug. "And I do have an older brother."

"Is that who you were visiting? In LA, I mean."

How do I say this? "Emmett, um... canceled on me at the last second. And by *the last second*, I was *at* the airport looking for him when he said he was too busy for Christmas this year." I sigh at the very thought. Such a dick move.

"I'd say I'm sorry to hear that, but it seems that worked out in my favor, huh?" he muses. "I did wonder how the hell you got to the airport so fast."

I laugh. "I was already there." I walk toward him, sliding past to get my toiletry bag and pajamas to change into after a long, hot shower.

I'm busy digging through my bag when Nick asks, "What about your parents? Are they still in California?"

"My mom lives in Napa with her new husband and twin daughters," I say, glancing up to see the cringe on his face. "Dad moved to New York to lead some fancy law firm after the divorce."

"I'm sorry."

I shrug. "They tried. I had a good childhood. I suppose that's all anyone can ask for these days." He nods as I pass him again, my breasts brushing against his abdomen. My face heats at the contact—and size difference.

If I wasn't so tired, I'd already have a forbidden boss-employee fantasy running through my head. "I'll, um, try to be quick," I say, blushing as I scurry to the bathroom.

About that fantasy...

Nine.

Nick

THIS MAY HAVE STARTED as a ploy over rights to a family heirloom, but it's already crossing a line I'm not sure we can come back from.

My heart kicks up a notch at the sound of the shower turning on. *My fiancée,* I test it, repeating it over and over in my mind. She'll be by my side for days straight. We'll be in constant contact between showing affection and...sharing this space.

My cock weeps at the very premise of sharing my bed with her. Is that too far? Will she draw the line somewhere? My guilty conscience starts to weigh on me as I spare a glance toward the loveseat beneath the windowsill. It'd be cold sleeping there, that's for sure, but it'd be the gentlemanly thing to do, right?

We're both adults, I reason as a bottle of lotion sitting beside the sofa catches my eye. I grab it, tossing it in a drawer in my closet. It's not exactly sexy, late-night conversation if I have to explain how my feet crack in the winter months.

I should probably ask her if she's comfortable sharing a bed before I start thinking with my dick. I scan the room one more time to make sure there isn't anything that could embarrass me when the sound of the shower turning off has my stomach fluttering—the same way it did when we kissed in the foyer.

Butterflies, *again*? I don't *get* butterflies. Yet, when it comes to her, I can't seem to stop the feeling. She's...perfect.

For this job, I add.

Because this is one giant ruse and *not* a sappy *Hallmark* movie.

While I wait for her to exit the bathroom, I look through my luggage, trying to decide what's best to wear to bed. Scolding myself for not packing more. I usually sleep in just a pair of loose shorts. I run too hot at night to wear anything else.

I pull out a pair of grey sweatpants and immediately put them back. Too bold. *Stick with what's comfortable*. She won't care, will she?

Why the hell do *I* care?

I turn with my sleeping shorts in hand only to bump into Joy coming into the closet. "Sorry," she yelps, taking a step back and giving me an all too pleasing view of her wearing an oversized T-shirt—no bra, I note—and what appears to be nothing else.

I swallow hard.

"Just wanted to drop these in here," she says with a forced laugh, raising the folded bundle of dirty clothes in hand. "Bathroom is all yours."

"Thanks." I nod, moving past her and heading straight for what I deserve...an ice-cold shower. Unfortunately, it doesn't save my wandering mind from straying to thoughts of Joy wearing only a T-shirt to bed. Surely, she has something on underneath? Panties? Shorts? Shorts with *no* panties?

I groan, leaning my head against the tiled shower wall. My cock thickens at the very thought of my fake fiancée laying in my bed in only a T-shirt and panties.

If only it was my shirt...

With that last image in mind, I grip my cock in one hand and brace the other against the wall as warm water pelts my neck and shoulders. I stroke myself from base to tip, biting back a groan. I close my eyes, falling into the fantasy of my hand replaced with hers—of her kissing and nipping at my neck as she guides me into her hot, wet pussy.

The visual causes me to jerk my hips into my fist. I come with a shudder a moment later and my shoulders drop. I shake my head. I haven't come that fast since puberty. And to the thought of my fake-fiancée-real-assistant. I still have to face her and sleep in the same room.

I finish getting ready for bed. Leaving my chest bare and wearing only my sleep shorts. I take a deep breath and open the door, turning off the light as I walk out. The room is dark aside from the dim glow coming from the built-in lighting over the nightstands and I see she's claimed my usual side—the right.

She's tucked under the covers, her damp, brown hair cascading over my pillow. She doesn't move as I approach. Is she...already asleep? I walk around to the far side of the bed, turning off the lights before I lift the covers to slide in. Waiting to see if she'll move or say something—protest that I've suddenly decided to sleep with her rather than offer to sleep on the cramped sofa.

But she doesn't stir. Not even a little.

Her breathing is slow and measured to the point I know she is, indeed, fast asleep. I lay on my back and sigh, peering over at her to note she's facing the opposite direction. And I'm not sure how to interpret my disappointment. There's plenty of room for the both of us—three feet or so between my body and hers—and yet...I want her closer.

I find myself scooching to the right.

Two inches. Three. Six.

I move until I'm lying in the middle of the bed so that if she were to roll over, she'd roll right into me. I smirk, then frown.

You're an idiot.

All evening she's been by my side, since the moment she got off that plane. Why should it matter now?

I like having her close, I realize.

As close as possible, in fact.

I wake to a pull in my shoulder—only for it to register it's from my arm hanging off the edge of the bed.

The *right* side of the bed to be precise.

My eyes snap open and I lift my head slightly. The sun peeking around the dark edges of the curtains has me reaching for my cell phone sitting on the nightstand. Except, this isn't my phone. *Joy.* I sit up, staring at the lock screen. It's a cutesy cartoon reindeer peeking out from the bottom of the screen with a tangle of lights around his antlers that say *Merry Christmas.*

I smile at the thought of her going through dozens of wallpapers only to settle on this one. My smile fades when I notice it's almost nine in the morning. Did I sleep in? I haven't been able to sleep past five in months.

My gaze shifts to look around the room. The bathroom and closet doors are wide open and the bed is empty—aside from myself and a tangle of sheets. Which can only mean one thing: she's somewhere I'm not.

I leap from the bed and rush to tug on a pair of jeans, socks, and a hoodie, then head for the door. There's a panic in my chest as I hurry down the hall to the top of the stairs.

Where is she? Did something happen? Why didn't she wake me? Did she leave?

How the hell did I sleep so long?

The boisterous sound of my father's signature belly laugh greets my ears. I pause. It's been too long since I've heard that laugh.

I descend the stairs at a more reasonable pace and round the corner toward the kitchen to an unexpected sight. Everyone is awake and in the midst of breakfast. Rich, Leah, my aunt and uncle, my sister—everyone aside from my rat cousin and annoying ex.

My mother is too busy cutting fresh fruit by the sink to see me standing in the archway, staring at Joy. She's at the center of it all, flipping pancakes on the griddle my father got on Black Friday seven years ago for twenty bucks and refuses to get rid of even though they have one built into the stovetop. She's gesturing wildly with a spatula in hand, telling a story about how her father accidentally used powdered sugar instead of flour one Christmas when leaving 'footsteps from Santa'—she whispers so Tucker doesn't hear. Apparently, the presents were overrun with ants by the morning.

"Oh, your mother must have been furious," my mom exclaims, laughing.

"She was the one who handed him the wrong container," she says.

Everyone laughs and Joy's gaze finds mine. A slow, stunning smile lifts the edges of her full lips. The sun beaming in from the window behind her has her looking like a goddess still wearing her pajama shirt from last night—with the addition of a bra and sweatpants underneath.

My grey sweatpants that I'd tossed on top of my suitcase last night. They're rolled up and tied tight around her middle. I walk straight to her.

"Good morning," she beams as I come up beside her.

"Morning," I say, sliding an arm around her waist as I lean in to kiss her forehead.

My sister makes a gagging noise and I flip her the bird. My mother swats my hand.

"About time you joined us," Dad says, shoveling in a forkful of scrambled eggs.

"We wanted to wake you, but Joy said you haven't been sleeping well," Mom adds, setting a platter of fruit on the counter. "Have you been feeling all right, dear?"

My fingers flex over Joy's waist. She shifts out of my grasp to place a golden-brown pancake on top of a tilting stack. I glance down at her and she quickly looks away, blushing. How would she know I haven't been sleeping? Then I remember our conversation from yesterday. I suppose the better question would be: How the hell does she read me so well?

"I'm fine, Mom," I reply. "Just a few long nights is all."

It's the wrong thing to say because my father pins me with a look and a raised, weaponized fork in my direction followed by the spiel about how my health should be coming before anything—including DSG. He's sure to throw one last comment in once my mother takes his plate and he stands with a grunt. "Don't be putting work over your lovely wife, either," he says with a firm hand on my shoulder. "She deserves the best. And your attention."

Joy sits beside me, a steaming mug clasped between her hands. "He gives me plenty, Bruce. And if he doesn't, I'll let you know first." She winks at him and he chuckles, excusing himself to lie down for a bit before today's festivities.

When he's gone, I turn to Mom. "You sure he's feeling up for the park?" I can't help but ask. His color may have improved, but he's still going through treatment. I know it's a drain on his system whether he likes to admit it or not.

"If he wants to go, let him go," Natalie speaks up from the dinette table in the kitchen. "You only live once."

I scowl at her choice of words.

"Your father's been very good about telling me when something is too much for him," Mom says, wiping the counter in front of her. "If he says he's well enough to go, then we need to trust him. It's a beautiful day. The sun may even do him some good."

I huff. It's also below freezing.

The kitchen empties while I eat. Joy helps clean before my mother excuses herself to check on Dad.

"What's the plan for today?" Joy asks, retaking her spot next to me. She turns toward me, bringing a knee up to her chest. Big, hazel eyes watch me. She looks so...content.

"Why didn't you wake me up?"

She bites the inside of her cheek. "You needed the rest."

"How—"

"My dad says I'm good at reading people," she says quietly, tapping her nail on the ceramic mug. "He said I would've made a good lawyer, but that advertising was a close second." Full lashes lift in my direction.

My chest heats. Does she know? Have I been giving away some sort of cue the last day to what I've been thinking? How I've been giving in to this whole 'fake' fiancée thing a bit more than I should be?

"You're, um, quite the bed hog, by the way," she says, changing the subject with another sip from her mug.

I do recall waking up on her side of the bed this morning... I guess I should've left the few feet open between us last night. "Sorry about that. When I got out of the shower you were asleep before I could ask if you'd rather me sleep on the couch."

"The loveseat by the window?" she asks, eyes wide. "Gosh, no. You would've been so uncomfortable."

I chuckle at her horrified expression. "Were you, though?" I ask. "Uncomfortable, I mean."

Her smile is slow. "You're very warm when you sleep. And you're a bit...grabby."

"Grabby?"

She nods, laughing. "You kept pulling me against you, and when I'd try to get away—"

Oh, god.

"—you'd mumble in your sleep." She's beaming now. "It was cute."

"Cute?" I question, my face flaming hot. "You just said I assaulted you and talked about it. In what world is that *cute*?" Joy giggles despite all of this. "I'll take the couch tonight," I say. "I'm sorry I was...grabby. Did you at least get some sleep yourself? We can skip today if you're tired."

"I slept great, actually," she says with a smile. "And I'd like to know what we're doing before you try to talk me out of it."

I shake my head, grinning. "Every year, a few days before Christmas Eve, my family goes ice skating at the town park. We'll get dinner in town and attend the Christmas Tree Lighting Ceremony followed by a stop at Annie's for hot chocolate. Then we end the night with a walk-through of the holiday display of lights. There's music and food. It's usually a good time."

Joy's eyes are as wide as saucers. "Oh. My. God. Heck yes, we're going!" she squeals, leaping from her stool only to freeze. "But I don't have ice skates."

"They have rentals."

"I don't know *how* to ice skate."

I chuckle. "I'll teach you."

She does a little giddy hop and throws her arms around my neck. "Thank you."

I hug her back. "For what?"

She pulls away, shaking her head and smiling. "I just—" She stops herself and the excitement dims a little in her eyes. "I'm just happy to be spending Christmas with you and your family, is all." She gestures at herself. "I guess I better go get ready," she adds, leaning in to kiss me. Her lips are soft against mine and she tastes sweet and fresh with hints of chocolate and peppermint. My hand still resting on her waist tightens—begging for more.

My pleas go unanswered as the moment ends far too soon for my liking. She smiles and walks away.

No one else was around to see that kiss, my brain immediately takes note.

She kissed me simply because she *wanted* to.

And I'm greedy for more.

Ten.

Joy

THE PARK IS A winter wonderland filled with people and activities. There is ice skating and sledding, a snowman-building contest, games for the kids, holiday music playing over several speakers, and multiple food and craft vendors lined up.

My jaw drops at the sight of an amazing sculpture made of ice in the center of the rink. It's a plump Santa waving with a sack of toys hauled over his shoulder and his lower half stuffed in a chimney top—and it is *huge*!

I can't stop smiling.

As an avid lover of all things Christmas, I've dreamed of finding a place like this. I used to sit at home and watch cheesy *Hallmark* movies and get lost in the spirit of it all. I was so jealous of those actors living my dream.

Now, here I am, about to enjoy the Christmas *of* my dreams with the *man* of my dreams.

My cheeks burn under the thick knit scarf Nick insisted I wear to help keep my face and neck warm. I've got two pairs of socks on, a thermal long sleeve (at his demand), his hoodie (also at his demand), my new long winter coat, boots, hat, and *two* pairs of mittens borrowed from his sister.

Meanwhile, all he has on is a hoodie, jacket, hat, and gloves. *"I'm used to the cold,"* he said. I argued that he lives in Texas now and should bundle up, but he seems to be doing fine.

I shift in place. My toes are already getting a cold bite to them and we just got here.

Nick's low chuckle catches my attention as he steers us toward the rental skate booth. "I take it they don't have anything like this in LA?"

"Not even close." I smile over the scarf tucked around my chin. "This is amazing. There's so much going on."

He grins. "Don't worry, we'll walk around afterward and see everything. We usually do ice skating first before it gets too crowded on the rink."

I nod, holding his hand as we move up in line. My head is still on a swivel taking it all in when I see a certain someone talking to Mr. and Mrs. Davis. Or should I say, a 'couple' someones.

I squeeze Nick's hand. He was so stressed yesterday and last night. I want today to be fun for him. I admit, Eric is...strange, but Darcy is the one who reeks of trouble in my opinion. Yet, Nick hasn't seemed to say much about her. Although, his face says it all. I wonder how close she was to the family after their breakup? Close enough to meet Eric, I assume.

"Joy?"

I'm pulled from my thoughts to Nick's voice. I peer up at him. "Hm?"

"What size shoe are you?" he asks with a smile, making me think that wasn't the first time he's asked in the last few minutes.

"Oh, an eight."

He huffs. "Eight. Right."

I lean into him. "I won't hold it against you for not remembering."

"This time," he muses, and I smile.

Next in line, we gather our skates and head to the covered area beside the rental booth with direct access to the rink—and somewhere dry to keep our boots. We walk toward the bench where Leah is perched with a steaming cup between her gloved hands, while her husband ties his skates.

"Not joining us on the ice this year, Lee?" Nick asks, gesturing for me to take a seat. He kneels on the chilly rubber floor, loosening the laces of my skates as I take off my boots.

"Pregnant and clumsy. Not a good combination," she replies, giggling as Rich attempts to stand. He wobbles, his arms darting out to either side for balance.

"And…I'm off," Rich says, making his slow, inching way to the entrance of the rink. "I've got a max of three falls this year!" he calls over his shoulder.

My brow furrows. "A max?"

Nick grins, handing me one skate at a time to put on. "He tries to fall less and less every year. Last year he fell four times. This year, he's aiming for no more than three."

Oh. I suppose falling is a part of the learning process with this sort of thing, right? A spike of nerves floods my belly at falling flat on my butt in front of so many people. "Is it hard? For a beginner, I mean." I ask quietly, leaning down to tie my laces.

"Tighter," Nick tells me, brushing my hands aside to take over. He peers up at me as he pulls the laces as tight as they'll go. Near painfully so. How am I supposed to move my feet when they're this snug? Reading my mind, he says, "The tighter the better. Trust me. You won't roll an ankle and slice open your pants like a certain someone…" He side-eyes his cousin-in-law.

Leah huffs. "Three years ago, Nick. Three! And that kid pushed me. You saw."

Nick chuckles, glancing up with a pat on my locked feet. "It's not hard once you get the hang of it," he says, sitting down to put his skates on as well. "And I'll stay with you the whole time."

I nod, the tension in my shoulders easing at his promise.

"There you are." Darcy bounds in our direction. Pristine, pearl white skates on her feet—the complete opposite of the tattered tan rentals I'm wearing. She's walking with an ease I can only assume comes from *a lot* of practice. "Beautiful day, isn't it, Nicky?" She eyes me from head to toe. Her left eye twitches.

A cloud of steam puffs from his lips as he spares a glance from tying his skates. "Where's your boy toy?" he asks bluntly, pushing to stand before turning back to take my hand.

"Busy," she says, her chin raised. "Business stuff."

Nick snorts. "Sure."

I opt to take both of his extended hands to help steady myself on the thin blades.

"He'll be here later for the light show," she adds. Nick ignores her.

My feet wobble as I take a tentative step forward. I can see why he made them so tight. The control is better. "You got it," Nick encourages, releasing one of my hands that I end up using the same way Rich did—outward for balance. He leads me across the rubber flooring to the rink and we wait patiently while a father and son duo step out ahead of us. The dad goes first, turning so he can help his son. The transition was seamless, and I let myself get excited again. If a kid can do it, surely so can I.

"I'll go first," Nick says. "Hold the sideboard and we'll go one foot at a time." I watch his feet as he glides onto the ice, angling his toes to turn and face me.

I gape. "You made that look *way* too easy."

He grins. "It is. Now, come on." He holds out his hands as if I'm a child, but I don't care. My pulse is thrumming with excitement at watching everyone skating in circles and laughing. It looks too fun not to try.

I take Nick's hand in mine, the other clutching the short wall as I put one foot on the ice. *So far so good*. It's slippery, of course, but my confidence is already building. I bring my other foot out and—

My first foot flies out from under me. I yelp.

My knees hit the ice and my face collides right into Nick's, ahem, crotch.

"Woah—" Nick is quick to correct me. Strong arms slide under mine and hoist me to my feet. I cling to him while I try to get my feet to face forward. *Not* an easy task.

When I finally do, I look up...and burst into a fit of laughter.

A grin splits his bristled cheeks and he chuckles. "Let's try that again, angel."

Eleven.

Nick

I can't remember the last time I had this much fun ice skating. Joy is giggling her pretty little head off and I haven't stopped smiling for the last forty-five minutes. She's trying her hardest, but the woman has zero balance whatsoever. It's adorable.

We've made it around the entire rink a total of four times and she's fallen at least seven—including her face plant into, well, my dick. It didn't hurt, thankfully, if anything it had me growing before thinking. Her hot breath fanning through my jeans had me wanting to drop to my knees instead of her.

The memory dries up as Darcy zips past us for the hundredth time, twirling as she does. I try not to let her presence affect my mood, but it's difficult when she's intentionally showing off like that.

"She's really good," Joy comments, her forearm locked around mine as we watch Darcy jump and spin mid-air with ease.

I grunt.

"Why does she call you Nicky?" she asks quietly.

"Because she knows I hate it." I sigh. "She didn't start until after we broke up."

She nods, gliding with her legs locked as I push my feet to propel us forward. After the third time around the rink, she said she liked this better. And since I like having her close—as in, clinging to me for dear life—I've been coasting us along for some time now.

She's having fun, and that's all that matters to me.

"Why did you break up? If you don't mind me asking."

That's been the question on my family's mind for the last two years. They adored Darcy in the beginning. Until her true colors started to shine shortly after my uncle's sudden passing. "Nothing was ever good enough for her. She always wanted more," I say, muttering to add, "She still does."

Joy looks startled by this news. "But she's so..."

"Fake," I deadpan. "Everything about Darcy is a persona, a façade. Her and Eric are a match made in heaven, or hell, depending on how you see it."

She faces ahead, her brow doing that little furrow it does when she's thinking something over. I'm starting to love that look. And I feel like kicking myself for all the times I didn't notice it before. All the times I didn't notice *her*.

"When, um..." She hums, thinking hard about whatever is on her mind.

I chuckle. "What's got you so deep in thought, angel?" It's the second time I've called her that, and each time it's given me these damn butterflies in my gut. *Why?* What is it about her that keeps stealing my attention? She's got me wrapped around her ring finger. Quite literally.

I could have thought of anyone else yesterday. *Anyone.* Yet, she was the only one roaming around in my subconscious. Has she always been there? How long have I had the thought of being with her tucked away?

I come around the bend a bit faster than I should and realize a second too late. Joy's legs wobble as she fights to keep them under her. Then they're not.

The blades of her skates slip sideways and smack into mine, sending me down with her.

We land with a thud on our asses.

"He's down!" Rich calls out laughing, and I look over to find several members of my family watching with amusement. I don't usually fall, having played junior hockey for a time in my youth. I'm sure they're all getting a kick out of this.

Joy hisses, grabbing where her hip and butt meet.

My pulse skyrockets into concern. "Shit. You okay?" I ask, getting to my feet before reaching out to help her.

"Need a hand?" Natalie smirks, steering Tucker's red ice scooter rental beside us.

Joy grips the edge as my sister holds it steady for her to stand. She looks up at me, still smiling despite falling so many times, but her smile feels forced this time. I wouldn't doubt she's sore by now.

"I think I'm about done," she says quietly with the cutest scrunch of her nose.

I nod. Most of my family have been off the ice for a while. Rentals are good for an hour, and we're cutting it close to the dinner reservation my mother made for our whopping table of fifteen.

I *slowly* guide us off the ice. I pay close attention, this time, and try not to let my head wander any deeper into my feelings toward my assistant. *Tuck those away*, as they say. Thankfully, Joy's exit is much smoother than her grand entrance onto the ice.

We're under the covered area, peeling off our skates, when I ask her, "So, what'd you think?"

"It was fun." She blows out a breath. "A bit bruising, but fun."

I chuckle. "You did well for a first-timer," I say, gathering our skates while she tugs on her boots. "We'll have you trying out for the Maple Leafs in no time."

We find our group shortly after and walk the two blocks to my parents' diner of choice. Dinner is filled with conversation and laughter. The food is phenomenal. I've got a gorgeous woman at my side to enjoy it all. And when Eric shows up late, even he can't ruin my mood.

By the time we leave the diner, the sun is set and the street lights are on. The family disperses with a promise to meet up in our usual spot to watch the ceremony together. "Ready to walk around?" I ask Joy as she tucks her scarf around her neck and chin. "We've got another hour before the tree lighting."

"Ready," she beams, taking my hand in her mittened one.

We walk through the park at the center of town, stopping at various vendors selling everything from handcrafted ornaments and jewelry to homemade fudge and caramel popcorn. Joy stops at several, perusing and conversing with the owners, asking if I see anything I like. Her holiday spirit is infectious and I decide to indulge in a few of my favorite traditions.

"Buckeye fudge," she reads from the container I chose. "You were pretty quick to grab this one," she teases.

"That's because it's the best combination of chocolate and peanut butter you'll have in your entire life." I grin, taking the container from her and popping it open. I pull out a small square and bite it in half, offering her the rest.

She smiles as she leans in to take the bite-sized piece into her hot, wet mouth. Soft, lush lips graze my bare fingertips and a low growl builds in my throat. She must hear what she's doing to me as heat flashes in her eyes. Her bold tongue sweeps over the chocolate smeared on the tip of my finger in such a lewd manner, I suck in a breath. The image of her on her knees taking my cock to the back of her throat fogs my mind.

"Nick, Joy." Our names are called somewhere nearby, breaking the spell—for Joy, anyway. Not for me. My gaze doesn't leave her as she steps back, covering her mouth and peering around us as she slowly chews.

She turns back to me a moment later, swallowing. "They're waiting for us. We should, um, probably go..." Her words trail off, hazel eyes flicking between me and whoever seems to be waiting on us.

"They can wait," I say. My hand slides over her hip to her lower back, pulling her flush against me. My cock reacts to her nearness. Her perfume. Her rosy cheeks and bright eyes to the gasp leaving her lips. What the hell am I waiting for?

"What are you doing?"

"Giving my fiancée the attention she deserves," I growl.

My lips crash onto hers in a searing kiss that leaves me wondering if ol' Saint Nicholas could help convince a certain vixen to let me unwrap her this Christmas.

Twelve.

Joy

"Three... Two... One..."

The massive tree at the center of town illuminates with pure, Christmas magic—and ten thousand multi-colored LED lights. A near mile-long worth of wire connecting them leads to the sparkling crystal star on top.

I've been to New York City around the holidays. I've seen the hype of Rockefeller Center and it is stunning. This tree, however, is a fifth of the size and holds ten times the beauty.

Applause follows the lighting of the tree and a line quickly forms with families hoping to take pictures. Somehow, Nick's family ends up at the front of the line. "Hurry, hurry," Natalie shoos everyone into place, handing her phone to the next person in line to take our picture.

I try to release Nick's hand and step to the side, but he holds me tight, fixing me to stand in place with my back to his chest. "Smile, sweetheart," he whispers low in my ear, sending a warm chill down my neck.

Strong arms envelop me from behind and I blush. It doesn't feel right being a part of their traditional family photo based on a lie, but it's hard to give in to my guilty conscience when he's holding me like this.

Several quick shots are taken before everyone moves along to allow others their turn. "We're going to head home," Natalie says, tugging Tucker's hat down to cover his ears. They give their hugs and 'see you in the morning' to everyone. Martina mans the stroller as they make their way to the parking lot. Nick's aunt and uncle follow suit. His grandparents are busy chatting with friends. Rich and Leah announce they're going to grab churros. Bruce and Betty get pulled into a conversation with their new neighbors, inviting them to Christmas Eve. Darcy and Eric linger nearby.

"Well." Nick grins down at me, offering his arm. "How do churros and hot chocolate sound, followed by a walk through the holiday light display?"

I beam. "I think you'd be a man after my own heart with an offer like that, Mr. Davis."

His eyes sparkle from the nearby Christmas tree and I fall a little deeper into him. "Then I'd say my plan is working perfectly." He winks.

I blush. Since this morning, my fake fiancé has been putting on the charm. If anything, he turned up to eleven, and boy, am I falling for it big time. His cheeky grin and sultry gaze. I sigh wistfully remembering the feeling of his hard chest pressed against my back when I woke up this morning. There's nothing quite like being the littlest little spoon to a hunky man who is a foot taller than you.

Nick pays for our late-night treat and we walk toward the entrance to the light show. We stop to watch a group of judges (since apparently there's a contest) declare the winners of the 'traditional display category' being that of over *thirty* vintage outdoor pieces. From Santa and Mrs. Claus to the original cartoon Frosty the Snowman and Rudolf.

"Looks more like a hoarder's holiday collection to me," Nick mumbles, taking a sip from his cup.

"It's a collection of memories," I say, cringing as the creepy neon blue eyes of one of the Santas stares deep into my soul. "An old one."

We continue making our slow way through the maze of lights and inflatable displays. We're a little over halfway when it begins to snow. At the end, we step into a wire tunnel covered in hundreds, if not thousands, of traditional white lights.

I hug the steaming paper cup in my hands to my chest, gazing overhead. "It's beautiful," I say. The warm glow is radiant against the falling snow. Far prettier than any big screen could emulate.

"It is," Nick comments, but when I glance in his direction, I find his attention isn't on the lights or the snow. It's on me.

My pulse quickens as he leans in, my eyes fluttering close in anticipation of—

"Excuse me. Would you mind taking a picture for us?"

The spell breaks.

After helping a couple get some photos, they kindly take ours in return before we begin the chilly walk back to where we'd parked—on the other side of the park. When we reach the sidewalk that leads to Nick's rental, he runs into a couple of old friends from high school. I opt to excuse myself to find a restroom while they catch up.

Trailing my way back to where I left Nick last, I see his dad, Bruce, perched on a bench outside Annie's Bakery. He's hunched over and his breath is coming out in quick heavy puffs like he just ran a marathon.

"Hey, there." I wave as I approach. "Fancy seeing you here."

His gaze lifts, but only for a moment. "Joy," he pants, patting the bench beside him. "How...are...you?"

"I'm fine," I say carefully as I sit. "How are you?"

He coughs, attempting to clear his throat. "Goo—Good," he forces out, then shakes his head with a swipe of his chin, leaving a pinkish smear there.

My concern heightens. "Are you sure?" I press further. He's rather pale, but the temperature has dropped significantly since the sun set an hour ago. I looked rather ghostly in the mirror myself a moment ago. "Can I get you anything? Water?"

He harrumphs. "You know, I never liked when people worried about me before the cancer," he admits, sparing me a glance as he adds, "I hate it even more now."

I smile in sympathy. "I'm sorry you have to go through this."

"Luck of the draw," he muses. "Once—" He starts coughing heavily. This one goes from rough, like the sound of rattling rocks, and then turns wet.

I quickly grab the few napkins I stashed in my pocket and hold them out to him. He takes them, nodding as he fights through a coughing fit from hell. When the white of the napkin turns red, my concern morphs into fear. "Mr. Davis? Bruce, are you okay?"

He tries to wave me off, but I can tell he's having a hard time catching his breath. His face goes from pale to red to purple in a matter of seconds. I drop to my knees in front of him, scrambling to help. I look around, not seeing Nick or his mom—or anyone for that matter.

Panic flares in my chest. I don't know what to do.

"Help! We need help over here!"

Thirteen.

Nick

"And what about you?" Mark prods, lifting his chin to where Joy excused herself. "I see you're not spending the holidays alone this year."

"Pfft. He probably has all those Texan women throwing their trucks in park to get a whiff of whatever fancy cologne he rolls himself in from head to toe." Todd leans in, pretending to sniff my shoulder.

I shove him away, chuckling, "Get outta here with that."

He barks a laugh. "Oh, yeah. They come at you strong, don't they."

Mark shakes his head at his younger brother, nodding in my direction. "You look happy, though. It's been a while. We should catch up. Bring your girl over for New Year's if you're still around.

Chrissy would love to see you." He jerks a thumb in his brother's direction. "She could use a new girlfriend to chat with."

I shove my hands in my pockets. "Yeah." I grin, wondering what Joy would think about staying an extra week. Would she go for it? I mean, she seems to be enjoying herself so far. We've gotten over the hurdle of sharing a bed.

My groin throbs at the reminder.

She's been out of sight for all of ten minutes and I miss her. What does that say about me? About us? I'd argue there is 'no us,' but between the butterflies and the twitch in my leg to walk away and find her...it's not looking good for me. I want nothing more than to get her back to the house, lay her down, and show her exactly how she makes me feel.

I clear my throat. "I'll give you a shout if we decide to stay."

A commotion from behind has the three of us turning.

Two paramedics sprint down the sidewalk.

"All right, well, it was good seeing you, man." Mark claps me on the shoulder. "Don't be a stranger."

I say goodbye and head off to find Joy. Oddly enough in the same direction as the paramedics went a second ago. Ambulance lights catch my attention out of the corner of my eye as they take the long loop around the park...heading this way.

An uncomfortable feeling replaces my thoughts of Joy and settles heavy in my gut. I pick up the pace and weave through the onlookers in time to see my father receiving oxygen from one of the medics. Time stops.

Joy is sitting beside him. Her hand is on his back where a heavy blanket has been draped as she speaks to one of the paramedics.

"Dad!" I jog to his side. "What happened?"

I quickly learn that my father was short of breath and coughed up a significant amount of blood. Medical terms are thrown at me like *hemoptysis* and *pulmonary edema*, until the ambulance arrives and a cart is removed. The paramedics help my father to stand and get him onto the stretcher.

I watch, a lump in my throat, as he clutches Joy's hand, refusing to let go as they wheel him toward the ambulance. "We're going to transport him to St. Mavis Memorial for further evaluation," one of the medics informs me. "We have room for one more if you'd like to ride with him."

I shake my head, fishing out my phone. "I need to find my mother. She's here...somewhere. She should—" The same helpless feeling I had when Dad was diagnosed engulfs me in a fog that I can't seem to fight my way out of.

I feel like a fish out of water gasping for air.

My dad is in that ambulance.

Joy's gentle voice consumes my racing thoughts and soothes my rapid pulse, "Go with him. I'll find Betty and we'll meet you at the hospital."

"A-Are you sure? I can—"

"We'll be right behind you," she says softly. "I promise."

I hand her the keys to my rental and pause. She stares up at me with those big, knowing eyes and I brace for the fall.

Because it's happening.

Whether she knows it or not.

My arms wrap around her and I hold her tight to my chest. "Thank you," is all I can say. It doesn't feel like enough to express how grateful I am for her at this moment.

I kiss her cold cheek and climb inside the ambulance.

When we arrive at the hospital, my father is whisked away for several tests. Thankfully, Joy and my mother arrive a half hour later and Mom takes over—seeming to know every nurse and doctor by name.

A doctor later announces he'd like to keep Dad overnight for observation and Mom opts to stay with him. We make plans for me to return in the morning to either swap places with her or drive the three of us home.

I'm hoping for the latter.

By the time we get back to the house, it's after midnight. I kill the engine and glance over to the passenger seat where Joy's fallen asleep. I find myself watching her—once again—but not having the heart to wake her just yet.

The moment is short-lived as she rouses slowly, her head lifting. She blinks in my direction. "Hey." Her smile is small as she sits up to gather our things from the day.

My tongue feels tied without a response. I get out and walk to her side to open her door. I carry the bag of fudge and take her hand as we head inside. We're silent as we leave our boots and coats by the door and make our way upstairs. The same routine from last night follows as she takes the bathroom first, then myself.

This time, however, she's wide awake when I come out of the bathroom. My chest bare. I flex for a brief moment under her gaze, then call myself an idiot for even doing so. After the last few hours, the thought of trying to impress her feels...juvenile.

I'm about to climb into bed when I spare a glance at the loveseat and pause.

"I can hear you thinking from here," she muses as she settles under the covers with a yawn.

"Is it all right with you if I sleep here?"

Joy nods, flipping the covers back and patting the bed in front of me. I suppress a grin. I turn off the lights and get settled, lying down as she adds, "So long as you don't push me out of bed this time."

"I won't," I say, eyeing her. "But you *are* on my side."

She snorts, half her face covered by the comforter. "I think you mean *my* side."

I grin into the darkness as we fall into a comfortable silence. Meanwhile, my mind keeps me awake. I try not to think of how the day ended, but it's hard not to.

Chilled fingers graze my bicep and I turn my head to find Joy's moved closer. I roll onto my side to face her, then silently reach for her. The action feels natural as she slides into my arms. Her body flush against mine. Her breath fans my chest before she turns her head to rest it against me.

My hold tightens.

We lay like this for some time. The tension that's been wound in my shoulders eases as the weight of the day begins to fade away. Everything feels better when I've got her in my arms. Like it's all going to be okay.

And it will be. Because of her.

She has no idea how grateful I am to have her here.

"Joy."

"Hm?" She tilts her head, and the moment I see her lips, I lean in.

The kiss is soft at first, exploring. We've kissed several times over the last few days, but there's something different about this kiss. It's...more.

Her tongue tentatively grazes mine and my cock thickens. My need for her—any part of her—is growing by the second with every brush of her lips. The soft, almost shy, touch of her hand on my chest.

"Nick," she breathes.

My hips twitch at the sound of my name on her lips. All breathy and turned on. *Fuck*. Is she as aroused as I am?

I veer from her mouth to kiss along her jaw, making my way to her neck. She moans in my ear. Her fingers flex over my pecs with a scrape of her nails. The sensation has my cock weeping with precum. I groan against her delicate neck, inhaling deeply. My hand trails the dip of her waist, over her hip, and around her thigh until I grip underneath it. I nip her earlobe and drag her thigh to rest over my hip.

The erection tenting my shorts brushes between her thighs, and Joy's innocent gasp only fuels my desire. "I want to make you feel good, angel," I growl, kissing her neck while my hand slides under her oversized shirt. Her skin is soft and smooth, and growing hotter with every kiss, nip, and lick.

I capture her mouth as my fingers graze the seam of her pussy. The thin material of her panties is soaked with her arousal and my mouth waters. I roll on top of her, my arms bracing on either side as I pin her thighs open with me between them. "Say yes," I pant.

She stares up at me, her chest rising and falling rapidly until she drags me down for another searing kiss and moans sweetly, "Yes."

I grin against her lips. "Good girl."

The sound she makes at my praise has me wishing the lights were on. To see her flushed with need and excitement for me—*only* me.

The thought is possessive. And it turns me on like no other.

She squirms with every brush of my lips on her exposed skin. I tug her shirt up until her breasts are exposed and use my tongue to caress the hard peak of her nipple. I fondle the other, tweaking it gently between my fingers. Her hands thread through my hair as her back arches, keeping me in place and begging for more.

I pull away and continue downward to the sweet arousal waiting for me. I brush her panties to the side and my finger glides along the lips of her dripping pussy. "Fuck, angel. Is all this for me?" I groan at the feel of her. So. Fucking. Wet.

"Nick," she pants, "please."

Precum drips from my cock at the sound of her begging and I groan, tugging my shorts down. My cock springs free and I grip it tightly as I push my middle finger knuckle deep into her tight, weeping cunt. I pump my shaft in time with the thrust of my finger to give us both a moment of relief before I pull away to yank her panties down her legs and discard them.

The moment they're gone, her legs fall open in the most inviting way. I push her thighs to spread wide and drop my head. I lick her from her tight core to her needy clit.

Her muffled moans have me glancing up at her body to find her hand over her mouth. "Move your hand," I demand. "I want to hear what it feels like to be mine."

She does, and I eat her pretty pussy with vigor. Lapping at her folds, sucking her sweet clit, and dipping my tongue into her tight little hole. *Goddamn.* She gasps and moans and squirms beneath me. I pin her thighs between my shoulder and hand when they begin to shake. She grips my hair as she grinds against my face. I'm so fucking turned on by her that I find my hips thrusting against the bedding. The rub of the three-thousand thread count sheets can't compare to what it'd be like to be inside her, but it's the overwhelming presence of *her* that is my undoing.

The taste, the smell, the feel of her under my tongue...

Fuuuck.

I slip a finger into her, curling it to find the rough pad of her G-spot. The moment I do, she's arching off the bed with a cry of my name on her sexy as fuck lips. I pump my finger, suck her clit, and ride the wave of her orgasm with her as her pussy pulses around my finger, pulling it deeper.

I groan at the beautiful, sopping-wet sound of her release as she comes down from her high into an exhausted slump against the mattress. My finger slowly slips free and I kiss her thighs, hips, the top of her pussy, her stomach, working my way up her body until my lips meet hers.

The heel of her foot presses into my ass, bringing me flush against her. The length of my cock slips between her wet lips and I pump my hips, gliding it in the most delicious torture.

Joy's breath stutters as she clutches my arms. "Please."

I grit my teeth.

We shouldn't, a tiny voice in my head reasons, *this is already complicating things*.

My resolve breaks. I drag the crown of my dick over her swollen clit. "Please what?"

"Please fuck me, Nick," she gasps. "Please."

I preen at her pleas. It strokes my cock in a way nothing else ever has. "You need me, huh?" I grip my cock in hand, aligning the head at her entrance. "Is that it, angel? You need me to fill this pussy. Stretch you. Make you come on my cock..."

"God, *yes*."

Any ration of thought leaves me the moment I push into her. Raw, hot pleasure washes over me instantly. I sink another inch, two, five, seven...

She takes all of me, tugging me down for a kiss as I start to move. My fists tremble on either side of her as I begin pumping my cock into her tight channel. She feels like heaven. "You take me so good, baby," I growl.

She moans as I drag along the inner walls of her heat. Her legs tighten on my waist as her pussy flutters around me. I pick up the pace. I take one leg and bring it over my shoulder, leaning over her as my thrusts turn rough until I'm pounding into her. "Yes, oh—Nick!"

I watch her face as she comes on my cock. Squeezing me, her lips parted, chest pink, nipples hard, and her gaze euphoric. I slam into her. The muscles of her cunt pull me deeper and force me over the edge with her.

I drop her leg as I fall over her. She clings to me as I fuck and fill her with everything I have. My cock twitches inside her with aftershocks of my release. I wait a beat before drawing back. She sighs as I slide in beside her. Rolling on her side, I bring her back against my front. Our racing hearts beginning to calm.

We don't speak. I kiss her neck and hold her close. I know I should get up and clean us, but I don't want to leave this moment. Her breath eventually evens out and she falls asleep wrapped in my arms.

Everything feels better when I've got her in my arms.

And maybe, just maybe, Joy could be my *real* fiancée someday. It's wishful thinking at its best, but it feels good to pretend sometimes.

Fourteen.

Joy

I WAKE UP TO Nick slipping out of bed at six in the morning to head to the hospital. He tells me to go back to sleep, but of course, I can't. His hot body—hot to the touch *and* on the eyes—isn't here to keep me warm. My boss has been my personal heater for the last two nights and I'm slowly becoming obsessed.

We cuddled the entire night. Him, holding me in his strong, sure embrace...keeping me *warm*. Maybe the more I tell myself it was his 'body heat' that had me so, ahem, *damp* between my thighs this morning, rather than his hard cock pressing into my backside and the memory of his tongue dancing circles around my clit, I'll start to believe it.

Fat chance, sister.

I sigh. Last night was...unexpected. After the way the night ended, the last thing I could have anticipated was having Nick Davis between my thighs, working me over as if he knew my body better than myself. It certainly felt that way.

Between his hands and mouth and his thick, hard—

"What do you think of this one?" Natalie asks, holding up an emerald sequin gown that's longer than I am tall, and popping my blissful memory bubble.

We're out shopping this morning at the mall. A certifiable nightmare the day before Christmas Eve—especially for anyone who doesn't like large crowds. I don't usually mind them, but this... This is insanity.

When Nick returned this morning with his parents, I thought we'd spend the day together doing, I don't know, something else? I certainly wasn't planning on going shopping. Or having to wait another hour for Tucker and Izzy to sit with Santa.

I had no idea parents could schedule that sort of thing online now.

Nick, however, isn't here and neither are his parents like they'd originally planned. Bruce is on 'house arrest,' as he so lovingly called it. He got a bit too much cold, dry air in his lungs yesterday, according to the doctor. He wasn't getting enough oxygen due to a bit of a fluid buildup in his lungs—made weaker by the chemotherapy he is on. The doctor said he was free to go home and rest. They made a follow-up next week and all seemed back on track. But I could tell, Nick wasn't thrilled with the idea of leaving him.

He told me I didn't have to go, but I didn't want to intrude more. I'd rather he get some quality time in with his father. So here I am, trying to find a dress for tomorrow's big 'Davis Christmas Eve' party with Natalie, Martina, the kids, and...Darcy.

"Um..." I stare at the gown. It's gorgeous, don't get me wrong, but I'd have to wear nine-inch heels to even *think* of walking in it.

"Too long?" Natalie asks, holding it up to my chin. "Hmm. Gran might be able to hem it for you before the party tomorrow."

Martina laughs. "Leave the girl alone, Nat. You'll have plenty of years to play dress up with Izzy."

"What about this one, Joy?" Darcy holds up what, at first glance, appears to be a tank top, but is a mini cocktail dress—emphasis on *mini*—with so much cleavage there's no way I *wouldn't* have a nip slip under the mistletoe.

A forced huff of laughter escapes me. "Well, uh, it's not really..."

"Nick is a breast man," she adds, leaning in. "He'd go wild for a dress like this." She winks. "Ask me how I know."

My cheeks flame despite my shock. He is? I mean, I'm no expert on the man, but this doesn't look like something he would go 'wild' over. And he seemed a bit more interested in other parts of my body last night than my breasts.

"Annnd *that* knowledge just ruined my day," Natalie comments, returning the long dress to the rack with a shudder.

Martina snorts with laughter, muttering something in Spanish to her wife that leaves her in a fit of giggles.

"Mommy, is it our turn to see Santa yet?" Tucker asks, coming in with the save of the century as he tugs at the bottom of Natalie's coat.

She checks her phone. "Oh, actually. We should probably start heading that way." Her gaze finds mine. "Did you want to come back or try another spot afterward, Joy?"

"Sure," I say. Anything to get out of this store and away from the direction this conversation is leading.

"Who knows, maybe we'll see something in a window on the way," she adds, pushing Izzy, asleep in her stroller, toward the exit.

It's not long before we find the line for pictures with Santa. They're running behind, of course, so we wait. Darcy stands silent beside me and I can feel her eyes on me. Subtle, but there. And boy, is it awkward. Though, it doesn't need to be, does it? She's not my enemy. She and Nick were broken up long before I (fake) came into the picture. And certainly, long enough before she started dating his cousin.

"Nick and I bought some fudge yesterday," I say to my fake fiancé's ex-girlfriend. *Say that ten times fast.* I smile as her gaze flicks to me. "I picked out this amazing white chocolate raspberry and Nick got this silly named—What was it called? Oh! Buckeye. We got it from this sweet old couple who—"

"I don't eat fudge," she quips, chipper to a fault.

I quickly recall what Nick said about her. *Everything about Darcy is a façade.* I mean, who doesn't eat fudge? I opt for a different angle. "So, do you skate regularly, Darcy?" I ask. "You seemed like a real natural yesterday."

"Every year," she sing-songs, her gaze drifting to the jewelry shop window on my left. "I figure skated in high school and college for a time."

Tall, pretty, blue-eyed, blonde figure skater. *Little Miss Perfect, one might call her,* I shake off the bitter thought. No sense in being catty. Nick made it perfectly clear why they broke up and why he wants nothing to do with her.

"Nicky and I would go to the iceplex in Houston," she adds breezily as if it's no big deal to talk about their past relationship with me—his fiancée.

I intentionally ignore the 'fake' portion of the title.

"And what about you and Eric?" I redirect. "I didn't see him out on the ice. Although, I was a bit busy trying not to fall." *Insert innocent laugh.*

I watch her response.

Her cheeks and jaw tighten and her head ticks ever so slightly to the right. "Oh, it's not his sport. Eric's big into football."

I smile and nod, deciding to press further. "How did you two meet? I thought you and Nick were broken up before his uncle passed."

"Oh, we were together. And thank goodness we were," she says, her voice changing to fill with sorrow. She places a hand over her heart for dramatic flair. "My poor Nicky. I had to help him clean out his uncle's cabin, you know. He was *so* distraught that day going through his things. He was lucky I was there to console him in his grief."

Huh.

Tucker grasps my hand in his tiny one. "We're next, Auntie Joy!" he hoots, and I instantly melt. He hops up and down with excitement, telling me all about his plans to ask Santa for a skateboard *and* a pogo stick. I laugh when Martina makes a slicing motion over the idea of him asking for a pogo stick.

Darcy and I stand off to the side while they get their family photo taken. Izzy wails her little head off when Natalie hands her to Santa for a picture. I take a few candid shots of the chaotic moment on my phone when a notification pings.

It's an email from the airport about my luggage. I gasp. "They found it."

Darcy raises a brow.

I shake my head, beaming. "I lost my bag between Dallas and LA, but the airline found it. Finally." I skim the rest of the email. "They'll be dropping it off at the house this afternoon." I sigh in relief. Not only from getting my luggage back, but the clothes inside—including a few options that would work perfectly for tomorrow's party.

Maybe even something worth Nick going 'wild' over.

Nick

I HAND MY FATHER a glass of orange juice and set a bottle of water on the end table beside him. "Did you want anything else?" I ask. "Mom and Aunt Sara are putting together some fruit and cheese trays for tomorrow."

He sips his juice with a huff. "If I'd known being old and frail would get this kind of treatment, I would've aged faster," he grumbles.

Uncle Allen chuckles from his place on one of the two sofas in the spacious family room.

Their eyes are glued to the football game playing on the wide, eighty-inch flatscreen mounted on the wall. The warm glow from the sixteen-foot Christmas tree causes a glare on the screen from where I sit, but I don't complain. Getting to spend the day with my dad watching the game and catching up like we used to—even if my uncle is here shouting for defense to get off their asses and Grandpa Frank is passed out cold on the other couch—it's been fun.

The home team scores another touchdown and my family hoots and hollers at the screen. I can't help but laugh when Grandpa Frank snores louder—his form of celebration.

"What time will the girls be back?" Dad asks.

"Soon." Hopefully. I stare at the clock on the wall. 4:17 PM. My sister assured me they'd be back before dinner, but then again, it is the day before Christmas Eve. I can't imagine the time it took just to find a parking spot.

I wasn't thrilled with the idea of Joy going anywhere that involved Darcy without me, but she assured me she could handle it. Martina also pulled me aside and told me that she'd keep an 'extra eye' on the situation, much to my relief.

Rich and Leah join us in the family room a short time later. They'd spent the day visiting friends and doing a bit of running around themselves. We're in the middle of discussing end-of-the-year details for DSG—quietly, so my father doesn't hear—when Rich says, "Leah was reading an article last night about airport thieves. I had no idea how common they were this time of year. I'm glad they were able to find Joy's bag. I bet she's relieved."

My brow furrows. "They did?"

He nods. "We passed the airport van when we pulled in. I figured they must have delivered it." I didn't hear anyone knock. Unless someone else got the door. Rich must see my confusion. "We saw them pull out of here."

Surely Mom would've come in and let me know if they'd dropped off Joy's luggage? If she noticed it, anyhow. I stand and head to the front door. I scan the foyer and walk outside to check the front steps, but I come up empty. I try the kitchen where my mother and aunt assure me they didn't see any deliveries come in.

I'm walking back to the family room when I hear a pull of a zipper and a muttered, "*Shit*," from the dining room off the entryway. I round the corner in time to witness Eric attempting to open a piece of luggage with a purple ribbon tied to the handle.

Joy's luggage.

"Hey," I bark, striding to him with a clenched fist. "What the fuck do you think you're doing?"

He straightens, letting the bag tip over onto its side. His expression goes from caught to snake-like in an instant. "What the hell do you care, *cousin*?" he says, the last word said with a hiss of hatred.

I scowl at him as I reach for the bag.

He kicks it out of my grasp like the fucking child he is.

I'm in his face a split second later.

He's roughly five inches shorter than me, so I make it a point to stare down my nose at the slimeball. "Touch my wife's things again and I'll make sure you never see a fucking dime of inheritance, *Eric*," I sneer.

Eric's chest puffs up and he cocks a crooked grin. "Wife, huh?" His laugh is bitter and forced. "Far as I can tell she's just some actress playing the part of a doting *whore*."

My fist rears back before my mind has time to process the action.

I'm blinded by rage as my knuckles connect with his jaw. All the pent-up anger I've been holding onto for months exploding in a single hit. His body falls to the ground with a weighted thud and crash as he takes one of the dining chairs with him.

"Nick!" my mother screams from the open archway. She tugs me away from my cousin holding his bloodied face, groaning on the floor. Rich and Uncle Allen come rushing into the room.

I take a step back, running a hand through my hair at the scene. "Fuck."

"What the hell is going on in here?" Dad shouts, shuffling into frame.

I stare at him. *He pushed me too far. He insulted Joy. He was going through her bag like some fucking pervert*, I want to tell him. But I don't. His disappointment radiates from across the room.

"Go," he says, pointing to the kitchen with a stern expression, and suddenly I'm a young boy again. The one who broke his mother's favorite vase because he was throwing a football indoors when he wasn't supposed to. It was the first and only time I'd ever seen my father look at me this way.

I hate it even more now than I did back then.

When my aunt comes shuffling in with an icepack and first aid kit, I don't argue. I grab Joy's bag and head upstairs.

—*ele*—

"Nick?"

I sigh, staring at the running faucet in front of me.

"Nick—" Joy rounds the corner into the bathroom and stops when she sees me.

I don't know what she sees. I can't even look at myself right now, let alone her. I focus on the blood smeared on my knuckles from a small cut between them. The skin must have broken when my fist made contact.

She's silent as she closes the door behind her and pads over to me. She takes one of the towels by the sink and wets it. "Do you want to talk about it?" she asks as she gently wipes the blood from the back of my hand.

I wait until she's done before I say, "I caught him trying to go through your bag." She leans a hip against the counter, patiently waiting for the rest of the story. She's not so naïve to believe that's all that happened. "There were some...words exchanged before I..."

"Threw the first punch."

I cringe. "Yeah."

"What did he say?"

I shake my head, my fist clenching at the memory. "It doesn't matter."

She nods.

"I'm sorry." I rub both hands over my face and groan. "I didn't mean to... I don't know. He just—" I sigh, my hands and shoulders dropping in defeat. "He brings out the worst in me," I admit, struggling to find the reasons why he does, why I let him get under my skin. "I don't trust him. I don't like him. I hate that he's even here..."

Joy delicately crosses her arms in front of her as she listens to me vent about my cousin until it forms into another rant entirely. Involving my ex. I pace the bathroom until my throat is hoarse and I feel a miniscule amount better than I did before.

"Can I ask you something?" she starts, and I nod. After everything I just spouted off, I wouldn't mind hearing her thoughts on how I'm handling this. Poorly, I'd venture to guess. "When your uncle died, did Darcy help with anything?"

"She made a few calls in preparation for the funeral." I shrug. "Mom was too distracted with consoling my father to do it. Then there was the aftermath of hearing his will, cleaning out the house and his hunting cabin."

Joy nods as I speak, seeming to hang on to my every word.

"Why do you ask?"

She bites her lip. "No reason. I—" She pauses, opens her mouth, then shuts it quickly.

I chuckle despite my current state. "What is it?"

"Um, could I—I mean, would it be okay if I had my father look into Eric?" She wrings her hands together in a nervous gesture. "Maybe he can—"

"Any other time, I'd probably take you up on the offer." I don't know what she believes her father can find that the local investigator I hired couldn't, but now? It doesn't feel like the right time to be digging the wound deeper, so to speak.

Or punching it.

"After how today went, I don't think it would be the best idea." The disappointment in my father's gaze flashes in my mind and I sigh. "Not for a while, at least."

"Of course," she says, her face falling. "Sorry, I just...want to help is all."

I close the space between us, my hands resting on her waist. Joy's eyes peer upward, heavy lashes batting at my heartstrings. "Trust me, you already are," I say softly, leaning in. She lifts up on the tips of her toes, her arms circling my neck, bringing me in and eagerly meeting me in the middle. And her lips...

Fuck, I missed these lips.

I bend down to hoist her up by her lush ass, placing her on the counter and positioning myself between her legs—never once breaking the searing bite of our kiss. She smiles against my lips and I growl low in return.

Joy slides her hands down my chest before pulling away. But I'm not ready to stop. I kiss along her jaw toward that little spot below her ear that made her whimper—

"Nick?"

I kiss her neck. "Hm?"

"Should we..."

"Anything you want," I groan, inhaling her intoxicating scent.

"...talk about last night?" she finishes, and I pause.

I straighten until our gazes meet. "What about last night?" My heart is in my throat waiting for her response. Does she regret agreeing to stay? Did I cross a line I didn't know of when I sunk my cock into her tight, hot pussy? *Is it me?*

Her cheeks are bright pink and she bites her kiss-swollen lower lip. "I thought maybe we should, um, talk and, you know, make sure we're on the same page before we do...anything else."

Talk? Relief washes over me.

"You don't regret it," I say aloud without meaning to.

Her brow lifts in surprise. "No, no." She smooths a hand over my bicep. "I don't regret anything that's happened between us. I just want to make sure we're on the same page is all."

I grin, liking where this is going. "And what page is that?" I bite back the urge to call her angel and further give away where I stand. She's smart, though. It doesn't take a rocket scientist to figure out I'm falling for her faster than I thought possible.

She shrugs, coyly toying with the bottom hem of my T-shirt.

I chuckle. "I like you, too."

Her beaming smile before her lips return to mine is enough to cure any doubt I had a moment ago. We make out like a couple of teenagers until she stops me as I start to play with the waistband of her leggings. Her cool fingers wrap around my wrist and she breaks the kiss. "We can't."

At my exaggerated pout, she says, "I was sent up here to fetch you for dinner, not *be* your dinner."

I bark out a laugh. "And what if I'd rather have you?" I kiss her softly, tasting her with a slow glide of my tongue over hers. "I'd choose you over any meal, angel."

She smiles, her cheeks flush a light shade of pink as she playfully pushes me away to slide off the counter. I grunt disapprovingly and she laughs, taking my hand. "We can play pretend later, *fiancé*."

Joy tugs me along and I follow her willingly, a scowl on my face.

I'm not pretending anymore.

And it's about time she sees that.

Sixteen.

Joy

Everyone has gone to bed when I tiptoe into the kitchen, cell phone in hand. The lights are dimmed, giving the room a warm, homey glow. My hair is still damp and my feet are chilly against the cool hardwoods. Nick is upstairs taking a shower while I've...snuck away. I mean, it's not really 'sneaking' anywhere when I was told to make myself at home, right?

Coming downstairs for a late-night treat to soothe my anxiety and call my dad are two things I would do freely in my own home. That's what I've decided to tell myself, at least.

After an awkward, and rather silent dinner, Nick retreated to his room early. I stayed to help clean up before following him upstairs. He's been quietly moping over his actions. I get the sense he's disappointed in himself. Even without his cousin and ex at the dinner table, he couldn't seem to get out of his head.

When I joined him, however, I dragged my newly recovered luggage into his closet and, well, I could tell right away, it was broken into.

I use the term 'broken into' loosely since nothing seems to be missing, but it was dumped at some point. Nothing is where I put it, nor folded neatly. Even my toothbrush is out of its case. And, call it what you will, but I have a hunch it was Eric.

Nick claims he caught him actively *trying* to get inside, but I just... I don't trust it. And I don't mention it to Nick, either. With the gross image of his cousin thumbing through my underwear in mind, I dial my father's phone number.

I know, I know. Nick said to leave it be for now, but how can I stand idly by and watch his family be infiltrated by, well, I'm not sure yet?

"Hello, Joy," my father's voice sounds from the other end of the call.

I smile. It's good to hear his voice. We try to talk once a week at the very least, but sometimes work gets in his way. I don't mind, though, it's still more time than I get from Emmett or Mom. "Hey, Dad. How are you?"

"I'm well," he says. "How's California?"

Oops. "About that..."

Dad harrumphs on the other end. "You're not spending Christmas with your brother, are you?"

I sigh, opening the massive fridge and peering inside. The container filled with Betty's Christmas tree-shaped brownies catches my eye and I pop the top open, removing two before I close the lid and the fridge. "You know how Emmett is," I mumble, taking a bite out of one brownie as I shuffle to grab a napkin. "When he sets his mind on something, there isn't room for distractions."

"He gets that from his mother," Dad says bitterly. "He should know how to manage his time wisely by now and leave room for important events."

"Like spending time with his lonely little sister for Christmas?" I snort sarcastically, stuffing another sad bite of chocolatey goodness into my mouth as I walk toward the breakfast nook.

"Exactly."

I frown and take a seat by the window. "Thanks, Dad."

"You know what I meant." He chuckles. It's good to hear him laugh, he hasn't done it often enough since the divorce.

We chat for a bit, catching up on what's new for him at work, his plans for this week—which are unsurprisingly work-related—and when I might see him again. "After the holidays," he says. "I'm getting ten times the amount of work done with everyone gone. It's a wonder I don't fire the whole office and do everything myself right the first time around."

I roll my eyes, the action causing my head to feel a bit loopy. *Weird.*

I shake the feeling off with a small bite into my second brownie and a change of subject, "Well, there *is* a tiny favor I was hoping to ask of you," I start, filling him in on the bits and pieces of Nick's cousin and the odd dynamic that's built over the last year.

There is a rustle of paper from my father's end. I have no doubt he's taking notes. "And you think this...Eric, may have some unsavory intentions?"

I shrug to myself, leaning against the back of the chair. "I feel like the situation speaks for itself, don't you?"

He hums. "It definitely merits looking into," he agrees.

I relay the few details I have on Eric and Darcy. He tells me he'll look into it personally when I say this is more of a favor for my boss than anything else.

"Has he not done his own investigation?" my father asks.

"He did, but he said they didn't find anything." At his silence, I add, "It was a local PI, and you always told me anyone with ties to certain people or places are more easily swayed to avoid the truth."

He chuckles lightly. "You seem very invested in this, Joy."

I blow out an exaggerated breath, my mouth feeling dry and sticky all at once. *Gross.* It's hard to tell if it's my nerves or guilty conscience that are getting the better of me. I might not be telling my dad the *whole* truth, but it doesn't hurt to give him an added incentive... "I like him."

Dad pauses. "But he's your boss, sweetheart."

"I know," I practically whine. This fantasy of being Nick Davis' fiancée has me all messed up. It just feels so *real*. Like he's really mine. And I'm his. He admitted he likes me back, after all. That has to mean something.

It means he likes you, too, duh!

And he eats pussy so damn good.

My body flushes with heat from my core to my chest to my face.

"I don't want to see you get hurt, Joy," my father's voice rings in my ear, yanking me from the dirty memory of my boss' thick cock buried between my legs less than twenty-four hours ago. "But, if this is as important to you as it sounds, I'll find something. Closure or otherwise. I promise."

I smile faintly. "Thanks, Daddy."

"I'll talk to you soon, honey. Merry Christmas."

I wish him the same and end the call, setting my phone down on the counter in front of me beside a half-eaten brownie and a small pile of guilt.

"Joy?"

I startle, nearly falling off the chair at the sound of Nick's voice. He grins as he steps into the faint light of the kitchen. "Sorry, didn't mean to scare you," he says, coming toward me wearing a pair of flannel sweatpants and a loose T-shirt. Yummy as always. "I've been waiting for you for almost an hour. What are you doing down here?"

My eyes widen and I check my phone for the time. I squint, trying to see the blurred numbers. "Is that a one or a nine?" I question aloud.

Nick's hand lands gently on my forehead and I peer up at his furrowed brow.

He really shouldn't do that. He'll end up with age lines all over his pretty face.

"You feeling all right?" he asks as I lean into his touch with a sigh.

"Mhmm." His touch is warm and inviting and— "Are you always this warm?"

Nick leans down, his face level with mine. "Look at me," he demands, and I do.

He's so close I want to just kiss, kiss, *kiss* him all over. But his gaze drifts to the table and he straightens, grabbing the rest of my brownie and bringing it to his nose.

"You can have the rest," I offer with a smile.

"Joy," he says, sounding cautious for some reason. "Which container did you get this from?"

"The one in the fridge."

"Yes, but which one? The one with the Christmas trees on the lid or the one with Santa?"

"I'm...not...sure." I hum, thinking. Why does it matter where I got them from? Betty said to help myself. "The other brownie had green sprinkles on it if that helps."

"The *other* brownie?"

I nod, pointing to the half brownie in his hand. "That's my second one," I admit, then start to feel a bit self-conscious. "Don't judge me, okay?"

Nick's smile is slow—and devastatingly handsome—as he pulls out the chair beside me and sits. "Have you ever taken edible marijuana before, Joy?"

I guffaw at the very notion. "Me? No," I snort. "I ran track and field throughout high school and college. My coach used to tell us it would 'slow us down' if we ever used it—which, now that I think about it, I'm *fairly* certain he was lying." I don't know how any of this is relevant to his question, but the information spills from my lips without any thought. "Then I got older and all of my friends already had their experimenting phase with recreational drugs, so I was kind of the odd one out, you know?" I shrug. "And at that point, I just didn't want to do them alone."

"Joy," he starts, his tone almost careful as he holds the brownie in front of me. "These are my dad's."

"Betty said I could—"

"You ate Dad's *weed* brownies, angel."

Time stops. Or—it doesn't, but it sure feels like it does!

I'm...high?

Don't panic. Don't panic.

I panic.

Gasping, my hands fly to cover my mouth. "Oh my god."

Seventeen.

Nick

Joy's wide, bloodshot eyes stare at me and I can't help but laugh.

"Oh my god. Oh my god," she gasps. "I am so, so, *so* sorry. I didn't mean to! I just wanted a stress-treat and I came down here to call my dad and see how he was doing and, and..."

"Hey, hey." I try to calm her down, taking her hand in mine. I give it a reassuring squeeze. "It's okay. It was an accident."

"What do I do?" she asks, now gripping my hand in both of hers. "I've never been high before. Am I high right now? I can't tell. My mouth is dry and my head is a bit swimmy, but how do you *know* if you're high when you're already high? Oh, no. How long is it going to last?"

At her rapid fire of questions, I chuckle. "Relax. It shouldn't last more than a few hours." Then I pause. "How much did you say you ate again?"

Her eyes are suspiciously glossy as she sniffles, "It's not funny."

I try to suppress my grin and fail miserably.

"Stop smiling," she pouts, teary-eyed.

"I'm sorry." I chuckle. "But I promise, you'll be fine."

She gives me the most miserable, scared, adorable look and I can't stand the thought of her being upset over something this silly. "Here, I'll even join you." I grab the half-eaten brownie between us and pop it into my mouth.

Joy scrambles to sit up, reaching out to my mouth with a stuttering cry, "Nick!"

I throw my head back and laugh, chewing the oversized mouthful. "You said," I say between chews, "you didn't want to do this alone, remember?"

For the first time since I found her half-baked, she cracks a smile. "But I ate one *and* a half brownies. That was only half of one," she says, in such a way it feels like a challenge.

And I've never been one to back down from a dare before.

I get up and retrieve another of my father's medically laced marijuana brownies and shove the entire thing in my mouth. "Hm?" I mumble, spreading my arms wide as Joy giggles. I swallow and grin. "Now we're even."

Joy's laughter continues as she asks, "So now what?"

"We just don't talk like we used to. Ever since my mom and Dan got married, it's been weird, you know? And Emmett hardly answers my calls anymore," Joy tells me from our spot on the floor in the main living room.

I'm not sure how we ended up in here. Possibly sidetracked from trying to make it upstairs, but I'm not complaining. We're lying flat on our backs beside the fireplace, our heads positioned under the too-large-for-words Christmas tree my family somehow got in here, staring up into the thousands of sparkling lights and shimmering ornaments. A kaleidoscope of holiday spirit.

It's beautiful.

Almost as beautiful as her.

I watch Joy as she gazes above, not realizing that I've been staring at her since she began talking about her family and the life she left behind in California.

"So when you called," she continues, "it was perfect timing. I didn't have to sleep in an airport or...spend Christmas alone."

My chest warms at her words—not the weed. I'm pretty sure, anyhow.

"Your brother sounds like a dick," I say.

"Maybe it's me." She shrugs. "Maybe I expect too much from people."

I roll on my side to face her fully, propping up on my elbow to gaze down at her gorgeous face illuminated in a soft glow. "Wanting to spend time with someone you love isn't asking for too much. If anything, it's the bare minimum."

Her face turns toward mine and a flash of heat grips my core at the sight of her pillowy lips. It'd be so easy to lean in and kiss—

"Are you a breast guy?"

My brain rattles trying to catch up. "A what?"

"Boobs," she says, grabbing her own and filling her hands the way I did last night. "Do you like them?"

Hers? Hell yeah!

I clear my throat, shifting in my pants as I stare at how her breasts overflow her smaller hands. They were a perfect fit in mine, I recall. Full and soft. My cock grows with the memory. My hands flexing. "Uh, yeah. Yeah, I mean, what guy doesn't?"

She hums, rolling on her side to face me. "I always took you for an ass guy."

I subtly shift my now *aching* dick at full attention. "Why's that?" I manage to choke out.

"Because." She lifts a shoulder casually. "You always stare at mine."

I groan at the oversensitive feeling of precum sliding down the crown of my cock and fall away from her and onto my back. "Fuck."

"What's wrong?" Joy shifts closer, her brow furrowed, eyes still red and bloodshot. She props herself up to peer down at me, tendrils of wavy brown locks shape her face. "You look like you're in pain."

"I remember why I don't do edibles now," I groan, the urge to take myself in hand is becoming painfully necessary.

"Why?" she asks. Her gaze shifts lower to what my hands are attempting to block from view. "Oh." She takes in the sight of my tented crotch. The flannel pants I grabbed are proving to be a poor choice.

To my surprise, she places a hand on my chest, drifting south on delicate fingertips. "Joy," I breathe as her hand slips beneath the waistband to wrap around my erection. "Fuck." My head falls as she gives my length a few tentative strokes.

"Is this okay?" she whispers, leaning over to kiss the corner of my mouth.

Her grip tightens and I grunt. My hand finds the back of her head, bringing her mouth to mine. She pumps my cock as we kiss, and as her tongue dances with mine, she slowly pulls away.

I am a panting, heaving mess watching as she slides down my body until she's sitting, perched between my thighs, tugging my pants to free my weeping erection.

I'm so fucking hard right now it's laughable.

"Joy..." I want to tell her she doesn't need to, that I don't expect anything from her, but all that comes out is her name in the sound of a near plea.

I stare in awe as the head of my cock disappears between her lips. Her hot mouth sucking me in with hollowed cheeks. I throw my head back at the sensation as she pumps my length with her hand in time with her mouth. She continues to take more and more and *more* of me until I'm hitting the back of her throat and she swallows, sending bolts of pleasure through my veins.

"Goddamn, baby," I moan. "Fuck."

She hums around the girth of me—sucking me in and fucking her face with my cock. Pumping and sucking and *fuuuck*. I reach out, threading my fingers through her hair, urging her to keep going just like this.

My hips buck as she deepthroats my dick. "That's it, baby, just like that," I growl. "You suck my cock so fucking good, angel."

Pretty, hazel eyes peer into mine. And when she moans around me, I know I'm a goner unless we want this to continue. I jerk my hips back, leaving her hot mouth with a sloppy, wet pop. I grip my pulsing cock.

Joy bites her lip, her gaze heated as she stands. She hooks her thumbs in the waistband of her pajama bottoms and panties. Painfully slow, she slides them down her creamy thighs.

I want my cum dripping down those thighs. I want to see it. I crave it. I want to fill her up again and again. Over and over until her legs are shaking and her pussy is swollen. I want a piece of me inside of her for *days*.

She steps over me, lowering her core onto me. The glisten of her arousal catches the light just so and precum pools at the tip of my dick. "Get on," I growl.

I watch with avid eyes as my cock disappears inside her—one thick inch at a time. Her legs tremble once I'm fully seated and I take her by the hips, guiding her into a slow, steady bounce. Her hands are pressed against my lower abdomen to hold her position. Several pumps of her tight cunt around me and she's dripping wet. My cock glistens with her juices under the warm glow of the Christmas tree. *Stunning.*

She starts to ride me then. Bouncing on my cock with breathy gasps of my name, I reach between us. My thumb finds her swelling, wet clit. "Right there," she moans, picking up the pace. Her nails start to dig into my chest and the mixture of pain and her pussy tightening around me have me teetering on the edge.

Her legs start to shake and her momentum slows into jerky movements as she drops onto my length—seated to the hilt. Her core pulses and flutters, gripping me as I rub her clit and pull an orgasm out of her that sends me tumbling over the edge with her.

My muscles tense at the sensation as the buildup of my release passes the point of no return. "Fuck, baby," I groan. My cock pumps as I fill her. Joy's name on my lips.

She sags over me, panting and smiling. I chuckle, aiming to get up and—

I don't have a chance to recover before my length is free from her warm heat and something wet touches the sensitive head of my dick. I stare down as Joy runs the length of her tongue along the underside of me—our combined cum collecting between her lips as she slowly circles the creamy crown with her tongue.

She sits back on her heels, batting her lashes like a fucking vixen—as if she didn't just rock my whole world. I'm speechless.

The sound of descending footsteps, however, has both of us scrambling to tuck my cock into my pants and grab a nearby throw. We sit beside the fireplace under the cover of the blanket—Joy's naked lower half hidden from view—appearing as if we weren't doing anything reckless in the family room under the Christmas tree.

When no one seems to be coming this way, I tug Joy sideways onto my lap. Wanting—no, *needing* her close.

"We should get to bed," she says softly, wrapping her arms low around my chest. She lays her head on my shoulder and I hold her against me, not finding it in me to leave this moment.

"Five more minutes."

Eighteen.

Joy

A DAVIS CHRISTMAS PARTY is unlike any family gathering I have ever been to. There's food on every table, drinks galore, games for the kids and even the adults, and a dessert table that Betty Crocker herself would weep at the sight of.

And the number of family and friends is... Fifty? Sixty? I've honestly lost count.

Not everyone can be this lucky, to be surrounded by love at the holidays. A time that can be the most depressing of the year for some. I've been thanking my lucky stars for the last few hours that I'm spending Christmas here.

My gaze flicks to the other side of the room where Nick mingles. He looks so animated, talking with his hands and laughing. He has the ear of everyone around him and I can see the pure joy he has on his face being surrounded by the people he loves most. He's in his element.

And he looks damn good in those black slacks and navy dress shirt with the cuffs rolled up mid-forearm. He grinned when he saw the strappy deep blue dress I chose for the party—it hugs tight to my curves in a way that didn't feel exactly 'family holiday friendly' so I borrowed a cream-knit cardigan from his sister. He teased that we are a 'real couple' now that we're matching.

My heart swooned a bit harder than advisable by any cardiologist.

Getting 'accidentally' high for the first time wasn't what I expected—aside from being a tad panicky at the start. Nick stayed with me the entire night, though, and I felt safe. Even if he was also under the influence.

The way we talked and laughed and simply enjoyed each other's company...

I'm in love with him.

I fell for my fake fiancé.

And now I don't know what to do except...tell him how I feel.

Tonight, I tell myself. *I'll tell him tonight.*

"We're happy with two," Natalie tells Betty's Aunt Sylva who flew in as a surprise for her niece. I think she told me she was eighty-nine. But she sure doesn't act like it. "Martina and I don't want to be outnumbered during the teenage years."

Sylva hoots. "Oh, dear, with your history and genetics, you'll be chasing after those kids like they were you. Your poor mother didn't know what to do half the time. Karma, as they say."

Natalie rolls her eyes, glancing at me. She gestures in my direction. "And what about poor Joy over here, Auntie? Nick was *way* worse than me. Their kids will be bouncing off the walls or—"

"Swinging from the trees," they say in unison, laughing at what I can only assume is a story I have yet to hear about my real-boss-fake-fiancé.

"Woah, woah, woah." Nick chuckles, appearing to my left. His hand slides around my waist in a way that makes the action feel natural. I melt into him. "I thought we had an agreement, Aunt Sylva," he says. "No embarrassing stories until *after* we're married."

She waves him off. "Bah. I never agreed to such terms."

"I certainly didn't," Natalie announces, her eyes alight with mischief. "You're gonna *die* when you hear this, Joy. Go on, Auntie. You tell it best."

The sound of silver tapping glass has the spacious living room quieting. We refocus our attention on Nick's parents standing beside the fireplace with glasses in hand as if they're preparing to make a toast.

"Thank you all for coming out tonight," he begins, grinning from ear to ear as his gaze sweeps the crowd. "It's been a heck of a year as we all know, but even in these unsure times, life continues to surprise us. Today we have the honor of celebrating the future and all the *Joy* that is to come..." Bruce chuckles, raising his non-alcoholic beer to the sound of clapping.

"Ah, shit," Nick mutters from beside me.

"What is it?" I whisper, suddenly nervous.

"Now, some of you may have already heard the exciting news," Betty chimes in, putting her hands up in front of her. "We all know I have a hard time keeping a secret." She beams as several guests laugh. Betty waves for Nick and I to join them.

"They're announcing our engagement," Nick grits low for only me to hear. He takes my hand and tugs me alongside him to the front of the room.

My cheeks heat involuntarily at the reminder of last night in this very spot.

If they only knew.

"There's someone here tonight that I'd like you all to meet," Betty says, turning to her son. "Nick?"

"Nick who?" Rich calls out with a laugh.

The room breaks out in laughter as the wide band of Nick's arm wraps around my waist. His palm splays over my hip with a firm touch. My body screams for more—more of him, more of last night, more of everything that is: *Nick Davis.*

He brings me in flush against his side. "Not too long ago, I met this amazing woman." He gazes down at me. "She's everything I could ever want. Beautiful, kind, caring. She knows me better than I know myself, and it made me question a lot of things. For starters, how could I fall in love with this woman in such a short amount of time?" He grins. "But she made it impossible not to." My heart is in my throat. *Love?* "So tonight, I am happy to introduce to you the woman who stole my heart, my fiancée, and the future Mrs. Davis, Joy Bell, everyone!" he announces proudly.

Hoots and applause follow along with cheers of congratulations. My gaze grows glossy as Nick sweeps me off my feet for a kiss at the crowd's demand. He holds me close as he swings me across his front, dipping me low before kissing me. The kiss is firm and sure and far too short in my opinion. When he lifts me and pulls away, I reach out to swipe the bit of lipstick from his mouth. He smiles as several awes break out around us. I blush.

Multiple members of Nick's family approach to congratulate us personally and the party begins to return to normal—

"Excuse me. If I could get everyone's attention!" Eric steps forward, his expression unreadable as he turns to Nick's parents. "If it's all right, Uncle Bruce, I'd like to make an announcement."

Bruce raises a brow but nods—though his wife appears reluctant, casting a concerned look at her husband. Nick squeezes my hand from our front-row seats to...whatever is about to happen.

Eric shifts his gaze to Darcy standing poised beside the Christmas tree. "My love," he starts, taking her hand in his as he drops to one knee. Quiet gasps echo around the room as Eric retrieves a small box from under the tree. "Will you marry me?"

Nick snorts, muttering, "Creative."

I stifle a laugh, nudging him with my elbow.

Darcy puts on the show of a lifetime—clutching her imaginary pearls, gaping at the unopened box, and fluttering her lashes as if tears have begun to build there. "Oh, pookie bear!"

Across the room, Rich has to turn around, both hands over his mouth as he desperately tries to control his laughter. Leah smacks him.

"Of course, I will," she squeals, leaping into her new fiancé's embrace. Everyone claps at the sudden display of love. Eric opens the ring box to reveal...nothing but a speck of lint.

Confusion radiates throughout the room as silence falls.

Eric turns his attention to *me*. Holding out his hand, he says, "The ring, Joy."

I freeze, shocked at what he could be implying. But the cold demeanor, the look of triumph, and the clear ask, I have no doubt, he *knows*. My head snaps to Nick.

His brow is furrowed with an undertone of that hatred he has for his cousin lingering just below the surface. I can only imagine he has the urge to deck the smug look off his cousin's face a second time. "What?"

Darcy positions herself in front of her now fiancée. She rolls her eyes. "Your engagement is a sham," she announces, her chin raised with a smug smile. "Tell us, *Nick*, how much is your *assistant* making being here posing as your girlfriend—oh, I'm sorry, *fake* fiancée."

The party comes to a complete halt, the music stops abruptly with a scratch of vinyl.

Nick scowls, his hold on my hand painful. "You're out of line, Darcy."

"Am I?" She scoffs, crossing her arms in defense. "Show them, Eric."

Eric pulls a folded paper from his back pocket, handing it to Nick's parents. Bruce brings his glasses over the bridge of his nose, staring at god only knows. Betty reads over his shoulder. Her expression falls as it lifts to her son. "Nick?" she asks softly, glancing at me. "Joy?"

You could hear a pin drop on carpet waiting for a response.

I want to find the nearest hole, crawl inside, and cry for days.

Tears well in my eyes, my gaze locked with Betty's as I shake my head. "I'm so sorry. I didn't—" The words lodge in my throat, a choked sob escaping me.

Nick's hand falls to wrap around my waist, tugging me against him. Protective to a fault. Yet, the words needed to explain this—this ruse seems to be eluding us both. How could anyone explain what we're doing—why we're doing it? And his cousin just proposed in front of everyone...

This is so messy. I have no idea where to even start.

"We thought you should know the kind of person your son is, Bruce," Darcy states firmly, clearly not at a loss for words. "Allowing a stranger to come into your home and wear such a stunning family heirloom. An imposter tainting the sanctity of Christmas." She shakes her head. "What were you thinking,

Nicholas? Did you ever stop to think about what this could do to your father's health? The stress alone is—"

"Enough," Nick barks, his jaw ticking. The heat in his gaze falters as his father finally looks up from the paper in hand. "Joy had nothing to do with this. It was all my idea. And yeah, sure, it started as a lie, but it's not anymore. I love her—"

A commotion sounds from the foyer, a muffled, "*North Tree Sheriff's department*," has a gasp passing my lips as does everyone in the room. Did they call the *police*?

The crowd parts under the archway to reveal three deputies. "We have a warrant for the arrest of Billy Shoemocker."

Heads turn, people stare around the room until Bruce speaks up, "There's no one here by that—"

"Joy!" My father appears between officers, his gaze quickly scans the room. His grey suit is ruffled, his tie crooked, his salt and pepper hair mussed, and the worry lines around his eyes are deeper than usual.

"Dad," I breathe, stepping forward.

"Jesus, Joy," he says, his heart pounding against my ear as he pulls me into his chest. "I've been calling you for hours." He holds me at arm's length. "Where is he?"

I blink rapidly. "What—Who? Dad, what are you doing here?"

"Eric Davis," he seethes, his gaze lifting over my head. "He's wanted for several charges of fraud, blackmail, identity theft, and is up for extradition to Canada for second-degree murder." He points behind me. "There, Sheriff. Arrest him."

Two officers move in and all hell breaks loose. Eric—or Billy—makes a beeline for the patio doors, shoving guests left and right before he's tackled to the ground. Obscenities fly. Chaos ensues.

Amidst it all, attention is called to Bruce and Betty who pale at the revelation, needing to take a seat to gather themselves amongst the excitement. Their faces are a mixture of shock, hurt, and betrayal.

Nick and Natalie go to them immediately.

I stay back, watching everything unfold before my very eyes. This is all my fault. Several guests stare at me as Betty begins to weep uncontrollably, and I have never felt smaller under their questioning gazes.

I never intended for any of this to happen. I never wanted to hurt anyone. I only wanted to help Nick and his family and now...

Guilt and tears clog my throat.

I ruined Christmas.

"Joy," my father coaxes, gently taking me by the upper arms. He rubs them soothingly. "There's nothing else we can do here."

But he doesn't know I love him, too.

Nineteen.

Nick

Eric or Billy or whoeverthefuck is hauled into the foyer as Aunt Sara hands my mother a glass of water, rubbing her back. She started crying the moment she sat down and it is taking everything my father has to console her.

"W-We let a killer into this house, Bruce," she cries. "With our babies!"

Natalie hugs her. "Shhh, Mom, it's okay," she says. "You didn't know."

My father shakes his head, his face red in anger. "I should've listened to you, son." He grips my shoulder. "I'm sorry we didn't."

"Ma'am, you're going to need to come with us," an officer states, and I turn.

"Get your hands off me!" Darcy's voice is so high I'm surprised we don't hear dogs howling. The female officer has her by the arm. "I did nothing wrong," she wails. "He fooled me, too. *I'm* the victim here."

Another officer approaches with a file in hand and I stand. "My name is Detective Waters," he announces. "I understand Mr. Shoemocker and Miss Laine have been—"

"*Laine?*" I ask. "She said her name was Darcy McCaine."

Detective Waters makes a note on the paper attached to the front of the folder before removing a paper and handing it to me. "This was found in an email correspondence between Mr. Shoemocker and Miss Laine," he tells me.

I stare at the paper.

It's a copy of a scanned letter.

A letter addressed to my uncle dated thirty years ago.

My eyes fly over the page announcing the birth of *Eric Steven Mitchell*, my deceased uncle's true biological son. The sender claims to be Monica Mitchell, mother to Eric Mitchell, who went on to marry her high school sweetheart and raise my uncle's son.

What the hell? "Where did this come from?" I demand.

"I understand you dated Miss Laine at the time of Steven Davis' passing."

"We did. She helped arrange the funeral and...clean out my uncle's cabin." The moment the realization hits me my chest tightens. I can't believe this. She exploited this whole thing based on a stolen letter. A letter I have never seen, and one I'm willing to bet my parents haven't either.

I hand the letter to my father as he comes to stand beside me.

Detective Waters' expression is grim. "I am sorry to say that it appears Miss Laine saw an opportunity amid your family's grief. We're working under the theory it was a backup plan in case the two of you didn't work out. Gold-digger, I believe the kids call it."

"Unbelievable," I breathe, shocked as I process everything. Billy is a wanted criminal. Darcy set this whole thing up. And for what? Money? Gold-digger doesn't even begin to describe the manipulation nor the situation. This is unreal. I had my theories, and a hunch or two as to what was going on, but this is so much worse than any of those mere assumptions.

I truly have a long-lost cousin. And he has no idea he has an entire family that was so taken by the prospect of gaining a piece of my uncle back, we took in a scam artist in his place.

"I-I-I—He's lying!" Darcy whips to face my father. "I've been a part of this family for *five years*, Bruce. You can't possibly believe I would ever do something so—so heinous." She's wailing at this point. Her face is tomato red as investigators carry her toward the front door. "Betty, please," she howls, pleading with my mother who averts her teary gaze.

"Quit your fuckin' crying, Darce," Billy shouts from his place in the foyer. "They've heard enough of your bullshit."

"Shut up, you—stupid asshole!" Darcy explodes, sending a shockwave through the room as she tries to high-kick her foot into Eric/Billy's face. "If you weren't such a useless idiot, I'd be—"

"I think that's enough," my father booms, nodding toward the officers. "Take them away, if you will. I'd like to enjoy what's left of the evening without these imposters in my home another second."

Detective Waters relays information to my parents on where Billy and Darcy will be taken and that they'll be in touch for their statements in a few days. Dad shakes his hand. "Thank you for coming, Detective," he says. "I appreciate the urgency in this situation."

"Of course, sir." He nods. "Though, you should be thanking Mr. Bell. The man was determined. I can only imagine the number of favors he called in to handle this promptly for your family," he says. "Have a Merry Christmas, sir. We'll be in touch."

My father accompanies him to the door as the officers leave and the excitement dies.

I run a hand down the side of my face, blowing out a long breath. *Fuckin' hell.*

Rich walks over, appearing as shocked as the rest of us. "I guess you were right."

I was. Yet, the victory leaves a sour taste in my mouth. "It was all Joy," I say, gripping the back of my neck at the tightness forming there. *Joy.* My gaze sweeps the room. I don't see her—or her dad.

I hurry to the front door, assuming they may be seeing the imposters out as well. When I reach the foyer, my father closes the door as I reach for it. "Is Joy—"

"They're gone," he says.

Shock catches me off guard. *Gone?* Gone where?

My brow furrows in disbelief and I spin on my heels to jog up the stairs, taking two at a time. My bedroom door is open and I check the closet first. Her suitcase is...nowhere in sight.

If she had listened to me and left the situation alone with not-Eric and Darcy...who knows what could've come of all this. She saved my family.

How could she leave?

Joy is...amazing. Beautiful, smart, funny. She's all those things and more. I've said it before and I'll say it until I'm six feet under: Joy Bell is perfect and— "She's *mine*." The feral declaration slips past my lips before I can stop myself. I don't waste another second checking the bathroom or elsewhere for her things. I race back down the hall and stairs.

They've got, what, a fifteen-minute head start on me? Twenty at the most. I tug on my boots and jacket, scrambling to find my keys. "Where—"

Dad tosses the keys to the rental car at me. I catch them.

I stare down at the keys in hand before looking up. "I'm sorry, Dad," I say. "I should have never lied about Joy. This wasn't her idea. It really was all me. I had to beg her to stay and...she didn't want money or...anything." The more I say, the harder I want to kick my ass for letting her leave without telling her how much she means to me.

"You thought I didn't know?" My father chuckles as my mother comes to stand beside him. He wraps an arm around her the same way I've done to Joy so many times in the past few days. That now feels like I didn't do enough. "I know who works for my company, son. We just wanted to see how far you'd take it," he muses before his expression becomes serious. "You love her, don't you?"

So fucking much. "More than anything."

"Then I fail to see the lie," he says, opening the door. "Now go." His eyes are misty atop his widespread grin. "Your future is waiting."

I step outside, breathing in a deep, cold breath of crisp Wisconsin winter air. Light flakes of snow fall slowly from the dark sky and I turn. My family is crammed in the entryway, sending me off with smiles of encouragement to chase down my forever.

I don't know what I'd do without them.

I grin.

Twenty.

Joy

I DRAG MY SUITCASE and carry-on behind me, following my father through the sliding airport doors. Mariah Carey sings her famous chorus of high notes overhead and I sniffle. My heart is heavy as we pass the exit for baggage claim.

"I booked us a flight to New York," Dad says over his shoulder. His carry-on glides beside him as he checks his watch. "We don't leave for another three hours, but I'm sure we can do some damage to my credit at the airport bar, don't you?"

He's trying to lighten my mood, but I'm finding it hard to think of anything other than Nick and Betty and Bruce and Natalie and Martina. Was Tucker upset I didn't say goodbye before I left? Will Nick give his parents the ornament we picked out for them or throw it away?

I can't imagine they're thrilled with me at the moment. After ruining their party and all. I fight down the urge to cry. Again.

I give him a small, sad smile. "Sure, Dad."

We print our tickets at an open kiosk and head to check my luggage. Hefting my hastily stuffed bag on the scale, a sparkle on my left-hand catches my eye. I gasp, "Oh, no."

"What is it?" Dad looks over as I splay my hand in front of me. The stunning diamond taunts me with a twinkle even in the poor fluorescent lighting. "We'll mail it back to him."

I drop my hand to my side, eyeing my father. "Dad."

He shrugs, handing our IDs to the attendant. "Return it when you see him in the office next week, then." Dad drilled me the entire ride here until I confessed how I agreed to pretend to be my boss' fiancé for the week. He isn't thrilled I'm not being compensated, or with my lying in general. I wouldn't doubt if he sends Nick a bill for my plane ticket to New York.

Tears sting my eyes remembering the moment Nick slid his grandmother's ring on my finger not far from where I'm standing. It was the highlight of my year—maybe even the last several years, if I'm brave enough to admit it.

From the moment I arrived in Wisconsin, I've felt...wanted.

It's a feeling I'm having a hard time letting go of.

"I should give it back."

"And you will," Dad harrumphs. "Next week. When he's got his damn head on straight enough to apologize to you for losing sight of where his allies stand. And has the good sense to thank you for saving his family and billion-dollar company from ruin," he adds bitterly.

I sigh heavily, walking with my father toward security. I dig through my purse, searching for my phone. *The least I can do is text him*. I let him know I still have the ring and promise to return it as soon as possible.

I drop my phone back into my purse after I hit send and we pass the first stop in security before having to wait in line for the metal detector. The airport isn't busy by any means, but it seems a few dozen people are gathering for their late flights.

"*Joy!*"

I glance at my dad, shuffling a step forward. "Yeah?"

"Hm?"

"You said my name."

"I didn't say anything."

"Oh." My brow furrows. I could've sworn I heard—

"Joy!" Nick's voice carries through the echo chamber of the airport and my breath catches.

The ring. He's here for the ring. I tuck my left hand against my chest.

Dad looks back and freezes. "Oh, my…"

I take a deep breath and turn to face my maybe-still-my-boss and current-ex-fake-fiancé.

What my eyes land on leaves me speechless.

Nick stands panting on the other side of security. His chest is heaving and his handsome smile shines as he grins from ear to ear.

I'd like to say it's seeing him chasing after me that has me weak in the knees, but I may need to give some credit to the fifty-something members of his family standing directly behind him. They smile and wave, beaming as Nick dodges travelers on his way through the security roped line. His gaze never leaves mine.

Surely, he didn't need to bring his entire family just to pick up his grandmother's ring, right? Hope blooms in my heart. Is he here...for me?

"Go." Dad nudges me with a chuckle as he takes the handle of my carry-on.

Tears blur my vision as I hurry past onlookers, fellow travelers, and suspicious TSA agents. "Excuse me," I say upwards of a dozen times until I'm standing in front of him.

"You're here," I say at the same time he asks, "Where are you going?"

The corner of his mouth lifts, asking instead, "Why did you leave, Joy?"

My smile falters. Isn't it obvious? "I ruined everything," I say quietly, hoping he hears the regret in my voice. "I should have listened to you and left it alone. You told me to and I...didn't. I'm so sorry, Nick, I—"

"You have nothing to apologize for," he murmurs, taking another step toward me. The scent of fresh air and sandalwood fog my senses. "I should be thanking you for calling your father. Hell, you were right not to listen to me. Who knows how long this all would have gone on without you. I owe you so much, Joy. You saved my family."

"I still should have told you." I sigh, finding it hard to take his gratitude after seeing the look on his parents' faces. "I swear I didn't know they were coming," I admit. "My dad works fast, but he's not very patient when it comes to...you know."

Nick nods before peering past me. He gives my dad an awkward wave. "Nice to meet you, Mr. Bell," he calls out.

Dad shakes his head, tossing a dismissive hand.

Nick cringes.

"I really am sorry—"

"Don't be," he cuts in, finally closing the space between us as his hand rests on my lower back, the other circling my hip. His fingers flex. "I need to tell you..."

"Kiss her already!" someone hoots from the crowd.

Nick glares over his shoulder. "I'm getting to that part."

Laughter surrounds us as my body flushes with heat. *Kiss me? Does that mean...?*

"Joy."

I fight my twitching lips to keep from smiling too big. "Yes?"

He takes a deep breath. "These last few days with you have been nothing short of the best days of my life. I know what I said in the beginning about this being temporary, but nothing about this has felt temporary. None of it was fake for me. I started falling for you from the moment you said yes," he says, and my pulse quickens. "I see clearly when I'm with you. There's no dark cloud hanging over my head at what the future holds. And I can't imagine a life where I don't get to crawl into bed with you at the end of a long day." His eyes shine. "The only future I want is the one with you in it. I'm in love with you, Joy."

He loves me.

"Really?" I breathe, giddy even as the tears start to fall.

"How could I not fall for you, angel?" He cups the back of my neck in his heated palm and leans down. "You're everything." His lips meet mine and I melt into him, kissing him back. My arms fly around his neck and the applause that follows drowns in the background of the moment.

I break the kiss only to say, "I love you, too."

He holds me tighter. "Yeah?"

"Yeah," I whisper, popping on my toes to kiss him again. I know it's only been an hour or so, but I missed this. Us. Him.

"Marry me," he murmurs against my lips before slowly pulling away and dropping to one knee. The energy in the crowd shifts. Coos and awes and whistles surround us.

My eyes widen. "Nick."

He gently takes my left ring finger in his hand as if to give it a tiny handshake. "I'd ask you to take the ring off and do this right, but seeing you without it for even a second would break my heart."

My laugh is watery as I try to blink away the tears.

"Marry me, Joy. Be mine for real this time." His grin is lopsided. "I promise you won't regret it."

"I never regretted it the first time." I lean in, kissing him softly. "Of course, I'll marry you."

He smiles against my lips and lifts me in his strong embrace as he gets to his feet. "She said yes!" he shouts, and the room breaks out in wild cheers.

I blush, laughing as he spins me around twice before returning me to my feet. "You're crazy," I tease.

"Crazy in love with you," he says deeply, holding me close as our family swarms us with love.

Epilogue.

Nick

One year later...

I SIT ON THE couch at my parents' house, watching Tucker and Izzy tear into gift after gift. Wrapping paper flying left and right. Natalie gave up trying to catch it all after the third present.

My stunning wife is curled up beside me in her pajamas, my arm around her with her back pressed to my chest. Her hair is down and she put on a light layer of makeup first thing this morning—not that she needed it in my eyes.

She's glowing.

I tighten my hold on her. The nervous excitement is starting to get to me as the presents dwindle one by one. We've only been married for two weeks now, Joy was adamant about having the wedding in December, as close to Christmas as I would agree to without it being on Christmas Day itself.

"Woah! A transformer," Tucker beams, turning to Joy and me. "Thank you, Uncle Nick."

"And Auntie Joy," Natalie says, smiling as Martina hurries to help him open the box before he breaks the toy in his haste.

"Look who finally made it," my father announces, standing with ease. After finishing his treatments early this year, with astounding success, he was eligible for surgery. And I am proud to say, that my father is cancer free.

There is so much to be grateful for this year.

I stand as my cousin Eric walks in with his wife, April, and son, Michael. It's been a few months since we saw each other last, but we talk almost every day. "Hey, man, Merry Christmas," I say, patting his back in a quick hug.

"Merry Christmas." He nods with a signature Davis grin.

When the investigators helped us track him down—the *real* Eric (Davis) Mitchell—a year ago, it was a night and day difference from when Billy had shown up. My father hugged his nephew and cried. He looks so much like my Uncle Steve it's jarring. Mom says it was the family drive Dad needed from missing his brother to push harder with treatment.

I think he was just happy to gain a piece of his brother back. Why my uncle chose to never tell anyone of his son before his passing, we'll never know.

I stay standing as my cousin and his family join us, making their way into the grand living room. I take a moment to gaze around the room.

Rich sits holding his daughter with Leah on the floor between his legs. Natalie and Martina sit beside the Christmas tree, watching Tucker and Izzy play with empty boxes. Aunt Sara brings a pitcher of mimosas in from the kitchen. Uncle Allen dozes on the couch. My mother ushers Eric's son toward the tree, pointing out which presents are his. Joy's father helps fetch them from deep under the tree.

It's not everyone we wished to be here today, but it's more than enough.

"Ready, honey?" my beautiful wife whispers, sliding her hand in mine. I grin down at her as she bounces from foot to foot. My stunning, amazing, perfect—

"If I run to pee one more time, your mom is going to figure out the big surprise before we have a chance to tell her."

I chuckle. "Do you know how much I love you?" I ask, kissing her softly as my hand covers her stomach. *Eleven weeks, four days.*

She smiles, placing her hand over mine. "Too much, I hope."

"There's no such thing when it comes to you, angel," I murmur, squeezing her hand. "Come on. Let's go give my mother the arrival date of the third grandchild she's been begging for."

The End.

Thanks for reading.
Please leave a review to let me know what you thought!
xo,
A. Boss

More by A. Boss

Montgomery Brothers of Montana Series

Only by You

Wanted by You

Found by You

...more to come!

Note from the Author

Thank you for choosing to pick up this book and read it! It means so much to me that you chose to spend your time reading something that I wrote. If I could hug you through this page, I would.

I hope you loved this enough to come back for more, because I certainly intend to put more out in the world from the *Boss Babe Universe*!

Don't forget to sign-up for my newsletter <u>HERE</u> and receive your *FREE* copy of *Only by You*, the insta-love story of Clayton & Julie, prequel novella to Montgomery Brothers of Montana!

Are you a *Boss Babe*?

Join the *Boss Babe Universe* on Facebook, Twitter/X, and Instagram!

Acknowledgements

A huge thank you to my critique ladies and beta readers – Sarah (sorry not sorry about the Maple Leafs, LOL), Colleen, Alicia, and Jill - I appreciate all of you so dang much!

As Tucker would say, "Yeah. I have friends." :)

About the Author

A. Boss proudly proclaims to be a romance enthusiast who just loves love! She's a simple writer who found her love of writing and storytelling—and refuses to ever turn back. When she's not diligently spilling her heart and soul into a word document, you'll find her hanging out with her loving husband, two crazy kids, and two sleepy dachshunds.

You can follow her on all the social media platforms for updates, freebies, and sneak peeks at upcoming releases. Twitter/X, Facebook, Instagram – whatever your poison may be – drop by and say hello!

Everyone is welcome in the *Boss Babe Universe*!

www.ingramcontent.com/pod-product-compliance
Lightning Source LLC
Chambersburg PA
CBHW031603310726
48974CB00003B/790